AF541266

EXPERIMENTAL TECHNIQUES IN ENVIRONMENTAL SCIENCE

EXPERIMENTAL TECHNIQUES IN ENVIRONMENTAL SCIENCE

By

Dr. Abhishek Swami
Professor
Faculty of Science
Motherhood University, Roorkee
Distt. Haridwar (Uttarakhand)
(India)

&

Dr. Vikram Mor
Assistant Professor
Department of Environmental Science
Faculty of Science, SGT University
Gurugram (Haryana)
(India)

DISCOVERY PUBLISHING HOUSE PVT. LTD.
INDIA

Published by:

DISCOVERY PUBLISHING HOUSE PVT. LTD.
4383/4B, Ansari Road, Darya Ganj
New Delhi-110 002 (India)
Phone : +91-11-23279245; 23253475; 43596065
E-mail : discoverybooksindia@gmail.com
discoverypublishinghouse@gmail.com
namitwasan9@gmail.com
web : www.discoverypublishinggroup.com

First Edition: **2022**

ISBN: 978-93-88854-96-2

Experimental Techniques in Environmental Science

Printed at:
Infinity Imaging Systems
Delhi

Preface

Today, environmental issues are a great cause of concern at the global, national and regional level. Several universities, research institutions around the world are involved in research on burning issues such as deterioration of the air, water and soil quality, climate change, deforestation, dumping of solid waste and many more. But very less books are available which summarize the practical analysis of chemical pollutants in the air, water, soil and plant tissues. This book provide details instructions and methods for practical experiments of all aspects of the environmental analysis. The comprehensive coverage includes the chemical analysis of important chemical pollutants in air, water, soil and plant tissue.

The introductory chapter of this book deals with the basic concept of errors, accuracy and precision in chemical analysis. This chapter also explains how different errors can affect the precision and accuracy of the results of experiments and how these errors can be minimize to improve the accuracy and precision. In the next chapter it explains about the laboratory solution and reagent preparation from salts and concentrated acid and base. In other chapters, methods for collection and analysis of soil, plants, water and air sample are explained. This book is expected to be useful for undergraduate, post-graduate students of environmental science, agricultural science, and atmospheric science. It is also useful for the laboratory technicians and researchers working in the field of environmental science.

Abhishek Swami
Vikram Mor

Contents

Error, Precision and Accuracy in Chemical Analysis

An understanding of analytical errors is essential because all measurements are accompanied by a certain amount of error, and an estimate of its magnitude is necessary to validate results. "Error" is defined as the difference between the true result (or accepted true result) and the measured result. If the error in the analysis is large, serious consequences may result. As reliability, reproducibility, and accuracy are the basis of scientific analysis. It is impossible to eliminate errors completely, although can only hope to minimize errors to their acceptable size. However, before talking about errors you should have clarity on the terms accuracy and precision. Most of us believe that these terms have same meaning.

ACCURACY

Accuracy is defined as the closeness of measured value to a standard/true value. Suppose you weigh a coin and noted 5.67g but its known value is 9g, then your measurement is not accurate. Accuracy is a measure of the amount of random and systematic error in a data set.

In order to determine the accuracy of a particular measurement, we have to know the ideal/true/accepted value. Sometimes we have a "textbook" measured value, which is well known, and we assume that this is our "ideal" value, and use it to estimate the accuracy of our result. A *true value* is that value that would be obtained by a perfect measurement. Since there is no perfect measurement in analytical chemistry, we can never know the *true value*. Even when we do not know the true value, we can rely on the best available accepted value with which to compare our experimental value.

PRECISION

Precision is defined as the closeness between two or more measured values to each other. Suppose you weigh the same box five times and get close results like 3.1, 3.2, 3.22, 3.4, and 3.0 then your measurements are precise.

Precision is a measure of the amount of random error in a dataset. It is found by measuring the same value on the same sample multiple times. Imprecise data will give a wide scatter. Precise data will be tightly clustered. Precision is a useful measure of data quality since it quantitates random error, but it ignores systematic error so it is not a complete picture.

Remember: Accuracy and Precision are two independent terms. You can be very accurate but non-precise, or vice-versa.

Imagine you are tasked to weigh a standard weight on the same scale many times. Because of error you will not get the same reading each time, but a spread of values. If these readings are a random scatter and they are not particularly close to the true value then this data set is imprecise and inaccurate because the readings are widely scattered and far from the true value.

If the readings form a tight cluster around the true value, but their center is far from the true value, this dataset is said to be precise but inaccurate. It is precise because the scatter in the data is small and the points cluster tightly together.

If the readings form a tight cluster around center, his data is precise because the spread of the readings is small, and it is accurate also because the points cluster tightly around the true value. This is the ideal situation.

Accuracy is a better measure of data quality than precision since it incorporates both random and systematic error.

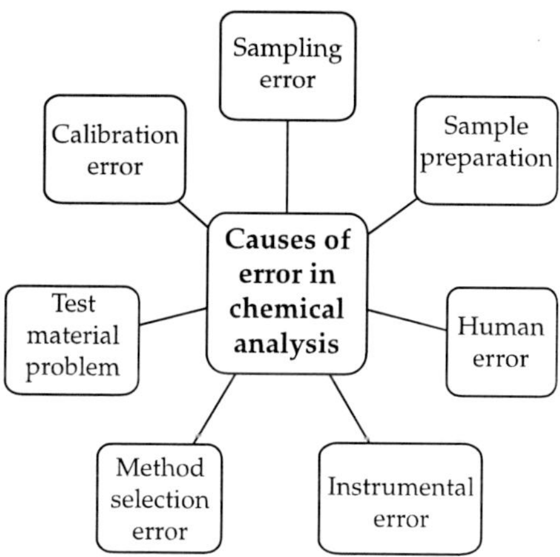

TYPES OF ERROR

In a general manner, errors are basically of two types:

- Systematic/Determinate Errors
- Random/Indeterminate Errors

Systematic/Determinate Errors

Errors which can be avoided or whose magnitude can be determined is called as systemic errors. It can be determinable and presumably can be either avoided or corrected. The errors which occur only in one direction are called *Systematic Errors*. The direction may be positive or negative but not be both at the same time. Some sources of systematic errors are as follows:

Instrumental Errors: The errors which occur due to lack of accuracy in an instrument are called instrumental errors. Instrumental Error occurs due to following reasons:

- If the instrument is not properly designed.
- The calibration of the instrument is incorrect.
- Degradation of parts in the instrument
- Power fluctuations

EXAMPLES

- If the markings of a thermometer are improperly calibrated, let's say it's 108°C instead of 100°C, then it is called *An Instrumental Error*.
- If pressure of atmosphere is 1 bar and the instrument is showing 1.5 bars, then it's again an instrumental error

Errors of method: When errors occur due to method, it is difficult to correct. In gravimetric analysis, error occurs due to Insolubility of precipitates, co-precipitates, post-precipitates, decomposition, and volatilization.

In titrimetric analysis errors occur due to failure of reaction, side reaction, reaction of substance other than the constituent being determined, difference between observed end point and the stoichiometric equivalence point of a reaction.

These errors occur due to:

- No ideal physical or chemical behavior.
- Completeness and speed of reaction.
- Interfering side reactions.
- Sampling problems.

EXAMPLE

- If we place thermometer under the armpit instead of the tongue, the temperature will always come out to be lower than that of body, as the technique of using thermometer is incorrect.

Operational and Personal Errors: These errors occur where measurements require judgment, result from prejudice, color acuity problems, lack of observation skills in an experiment and are based on the carelessness of individual only. These errors are physical in nature and occur when sound analytical techniques is not followed. Personal errors depend on the user or student performing the experiment and have nothing to do with instrument settings.

EXAMPLE

- For measuring height of an object, if the student don't place his head in a proper way, it may lead to parallax and readings won't be correct.

How to reduce systematic errors?

Systematic errors can be downplayed by:

- Improving experimental techniques by performing experiment as per the guidelines and precautions of the experiment.
- By using correct, rightly accurate instruments and sending old worn out instruments for maintenance.
- Concentrating more while performing an experiment in order to avoid silly mistakes in taking the readings of the measurement.
- Removing personal mistakes as far as possible and keeping instruments safely after the experiment.

Random Errors

It occurs accidentally or randomly so called as indeterminate or accidental or random error. Analyst has no control in this error. It follows a random distribution and a mathematical law of probability can be applied. Random Errors are not identifiable, always present, and cannot be eliminated. Random errors occur due to:

- Sudden and unexpected shifts in experimental conditions of the environment.
- Personal bias errors which even the student is unaware of.

EXAMPLE

- A spring balance will give different readings if the temperature of the environment is not constant.
- If a person repeats an experiment he is more likely to get different observations.

We can only reduce random errors and can't eliminate them completely as they are unpredictable and not fixed in nature as systematic errors are.

Absolute Error

It is the difference between the actual and measured value.

Let's say a meter stick is used to measure a given distance. The error is rather hastily made, but it is good to ± 1mm. This is the absolute error of the measurement.

absolute error = ±1mm (0.001m).

Relative Error: Relative error gives an indication of how good a measurement is relative to the size of the thing being measured. Let's say that two students measure two objects with a meter stick. One student measures the height of a room and gets a value of 3.215 meters ± 1mm (0.001m). Another student measures the height of a small cylinder and measures 0.075 meters ± 1mm (0.001m). Clearly, the overall accuracy of the ceiling height is much better than that of the 7.5 cm cylinder. The comparative accuracy of these measurements can be determined by looking at their relative errors.

Relative error = absolute error/Actual value

2

Laboratory Solution and Reagents Preparation

Most of the reagents/chemicals used in science are in the form of solutions which need to be purchased or prepared by mixing solute and solvent. For scientific analysis, the concentration of the solution and its method of preparation must be as accurate as possible because the quantity of solute that is dissolved in a particular quantity of solvent describes the quantity of a solute that is contained in a particular quantity of solvent or solution. Knowing the concentration of solutes is important in controlling the stoichiometry of reactants for reactions that occur in solution. If you can do so, your chemistry analytical abilities become very good and you become an expert in making the solution as well as in the calculation of the solution and solubility-related problems. To prepare a solution that contains a specified concentration of a substance, it is necessary to dissolve the desired number of moles of solute in enough solvent to give the desired final volume of solution. Therefore, understanding the solution preparation is crucial for the chemical analysis.

WHAT IS SOLUTION IN CHEMICAL ANALYSIS ?

In general, solution means a liquid state of a substance in which another substance is dissolved. But in chemistry terms, a solution is a homogeneous mixture of two chemical/ substances in a relative amount. All solutions contain a solvent and one or more solutes. The solvent, often water, is the chemical that's most abundant. The solute is the chemical(s) that's less abundant. For example, when NaCl is dissolved in water then it is a solution where water is solvent and NaCl is solute. Therefore, in other words, the solution is a mixture of a solute in the solvent.

THE CONCENTRATION OF SOLUTIONS IN CHEMISTRY

In order to prepare the solution, first, determine the concentration of solution needed for the experiment. Therefore we need to know about what is the concentration of solutions?

The concentration of a solution is a measure of the amount of solute that has been dissolved in a given amount of solvent or solution. A concentrated solution is one that has a relatively large amount of dissolved solute. A dilute solution is one that has a relatively small amount of dissolved solute. To get a clear idea we can consider three glasses of a solution of sugar in water. The concentration of sugar in the first glass is less than the other two. On the other hand, the concentration of the third glass is more than the other two. So the concentration of a solution is indicating the amount of solute contains in the solvent. However, these terms are relative, and we need to be able to express concentration in a more exact, quantitative manner. Still, concentrated and dilute are useful as terms to compare one solution to another. Also, be aware that the terms "concentrate" and "dilute" can be used as verbs. If you were to heat a solution, causing the solvent to evaporate, you would be concentrating it, because the ratio of solute to solvent would be increasing. If you were to add more water to an aqueous solution, you would be diluting it because the ratio of solute to solvent would be decreasing.

Concentration can be expressed in several different ways:

- Molarity
- Normality
- Molality
- Percentage

MOLARITY

Chemists primarily need the concentration of solutions to be expressed in a way that accounts for the number of particles that react according to a particular chemical equation. Since percentage measurements are based on either mass or volume, they are generally not useful for chemical reactions. A concentration unit based on moles is preferable. The most common unit of solution concentration is molarity (M). The molarity (M) of a solution is the number of moles of solute dissolved in one liter of solution. One liter of solution contains both the solute and the solvent. Therefore, to calculate the molarity of a solution, the moles of solute divided by the volume of the solution expressed in liters.

Molarity (M)= moles of solute/liters of solution= mol/L

For example: Prepare 1 liter of 1.00 M NaCl solution. First, calculate the molar mass of NaCl which is the mass of a mole of Na plus the mass of a mole of Cl or 22.99 + 35.45 = 58.44 gm/mol.

- Weigh out 58.44 gm NaCl.
- Place the NaCl in a 1 liter volumetric flask.
- Add a small volume of distilled water to dissolve the salt and fill the flask to the 1 liter mark.

If a different molarity is required, then multiply that number times the molar mass of NaCl. For example, if you wanted a 0.5 M solution, you would use 0.5 × 58.44 gm/mol of NaCl in 1 L of solution or 29.22 gm of NaCl.

NORMALITY

Normality (N) is another way to quantify solution concentration. It is similar to molarity but uses the gram-equivalent weight of a solute in its expression of solute amount in a liter of solution, rather than the gram molecular weight (GMW) expressed in molarity. The gram equivalent is the amount of a substance that will react or supply 1 mole of hydrogen ion (H+) or electron (e-).

Gram equivalent weight of solute= Molecular mass/ Valency factor

The normality of a solution is the gram equivalent weight of a solute per liter of solution. It may also be called the equivalent concentration. It is indicated by using the symbol N, eq/L, or meq/L (= 0.001 N) for units of concentration. Normality is typically useful in acid-base reactions.

Normality=Grams equivalent weight of solute/liters of solution

For example: Prepare 1 liter of 1.00 N NaCl solution.

- The molecular weight of the NaCl is 58.44 gm.
- Valency of NaCl=1
- Equivalent weight=58.44/1=58.44 gm

Therefore, we required 58.44 gm of NaCl to prepare 1 liter of 1N NaCl.

But, preparing normal solutions from concentrated liquid chemicals like sulfuric acid, nitric acid, and hydrochloric acid is slightly different and requires few more calculations. First, it is important to describe a few aspects of concentrated liquid chemicals. Most of us buy concentrated acids to use as stock solutions in the laboratory. None of these acids are one hundred percent pure. Sulfuric acid is only about 97% pure, nitric is about 69.5%, and hydrochloric acid is about 37.5% pure.

Another important aspect of these solutions is their specific gravities. The specific gravity of a liquid is, in most cases, synonymous with the more familiar term of density. Water has a specific gravity of 1. The specific gravity for concentrated sulfuric acid is about 1.84 or 1.84 times heavier than an equal volume of water. The specific gravity of concentrated nitric acid is about 1.42 and that of concentrated hydrochloric acid is about 1.19.

Both the percent concentration and specific gravity values of the acid are required to determine the amount of concentrated acid needed when making a Normal solution.

Here is an example:

To make 500 ml of a 1 N H_2SO_4, how many milliliters of concentrated sulfuric acid do you need?

To do this, first need to calculate the equivalent mass of H_2SO_4. It is 98/2 = 49. Then you can calculate the amount of grams of H_2SO_4 that are needed.

The formula to calculate amount of grams of H_2SO_4 that are needed:

Grams of compound needed = (N desired) (equivalent mass) (volume in liters desired).

Substituting the above numbers into the equation, we get:

Grams of compound needed = (1 N) (49) (0.500 liters) = 24.50 grams.

A 1 N solution requires 24.50 gm of a pure sulfuric acid powder (if one existed) diluted to 500 ml. But the acid is a liquid and it is not one hundred percent pure active sulfuric acid. You will need to calculate what volume of the concentrated acid that contains 24.50 gm of H_2SO_4.

The formula for this is:

Volume of H_2SO_4 needed = (grams of acid needed)/(% concentration × specific gravity)

Substituting the values into the equation, we get:

Volume of concentrated acid needed = (24.50)/(0.97 × 1.84) = 13.8 ml

So, for making 500 ml of 1N H_2SO_4 solution we have to take 13.8 ml of concentrated sulfuric acid and diluted it to 500ml.

Molality

Molality (m) can be defined as the ratio of number of moles of solute to the mass of solvent in kg.

It can also be defined as the number of moles of solute present in 1 Kg of solvent. A solution of concentration 1 mol/Kg is also sometimes denoted as 1 molal. It is denoted by M.

It can be expressed as:

Molality (m) = No. of moles of Solute/weight of Solvent in Kg

For example: Calculate the molality of the solution prepared from 14.61 gm NaCl in 1 kg of water.

Molar mass of NaCl= 58.44 gm/mol

Number of moles of solute= 14.61/58.44 = 0.25 moles

After putting these values in formula, we get:

Molality = 0.25/1 = 0.25 moles/kg

PERCENT SOLUTIONS

One way to describe the concentration of a solution is by the percent of a solute in the solvent. The percent can further be determined in one of two ways:

1. The ratio of the mass of the solute divided by the mass of the solution

or

2. The ratio of the volume of the solute divided by the volume of the solution.

MASS PERCENT

When the solute in a solution is a solid, a convenient way to express the concentration is by mass percent (mass/mass), which is the grams of solute per 100gm of solution.

% by mass= (mass of solute/mass of solution)×100%

Suppose that a solution was prepared by dissolving 50gm of sugar into 200g of water. The percent by mass would be calculated by:

Percent by mass = (50gm sugar/250gm solution) × 100% = 20% sugar

Sometimes you may want to make up a particular mass of solution of a given percent by mass, and need to calculate what mass of the solvent to use. For example, you need to make 2000gm of a 5% solution of sodium chloride. You can rearrange and solve for the mass of solute:

Mass of solute = (percent by mass/100%) × mass of solution

= (5/100) × 2000gm =100gm NaCl

You would need to weigh out 100 gm of NaCl and add it to 2900 gm of water.

VOLUME PERCENT

The percentage of solute in a solution can more easily be determined by volume when the solute and solvent are both liquids. The volume of the solute divided by the volume of the solution, expressed as a percent, yields the percent by volume (volume/volume) of the solution. If a solution is made by adding 80mL of ethanol to 200 ml of water, the percent by volume is:

Percent by volume = (volume of solute/volume of solution) × 100%

= 80ml ethanol/280ml solution × 100%

= 28.57% ethanol

DILUTIONS OF SOLUTIONS

Dilutions play a crucial role in quantitative estimations. Whenever the concentration of the analyte in a sample is high then requires a single or multi stage dilution before estimation. Similarly dilutions are essential for preparing standard solutions for generation of calibration plots. Diluting a solution involves adding additional solvent to decrease the solution's concentration. For example, you can add more water to sugar syrup to dilute it and reduce the strength of sugar in the entire mixture.

The volume of solvent needed to prepare the desired concentration of a new, diluted solution can be calculated mathematically. The relationship is as follows:

M1V1=M2V2

where:

M1 denotes the concentration of the original solution, and V1 denotes the volume of the original solution; M2 represents the concentration of the diluted solution, and V2 represents the final volume of the diluted solution. When calculating dilution factors, it is important that the units for both volume and concentration are the same for both sides of the equation.

For example: If 200 mL of a 1.5 M aqueous solution of NaCl is diluted with water to a final volume of 1.0 L. What is the final concentration of the diluted solution?

M1V1=M2V2

(1.5 M)(200 mL) = M2 (1000 mL)

M2 = 0.3 M

3

Soil Analysis

SCOPE AND APPLICATION

The purpose of this standard operating procedure (SOP) is to describe the procedures for the sampling of soil both in field and in laboratory. The soil inherently posses large heterogeneity. This causes problem in getting representative sample. The method and procedure for obtaining soil samples vary according to the purpose of sampling. Soils vary from place to place. In view of this, efforts should be made to take the samples in such a way that it fully represents the field.

PROCEDURE

(a) Sampling of soil from the field

Materials like weeds, stubble and other unwanted substances are removed from the sampling point prior to taking the sample.

Demarcate the field to be surveyed into uniform portions (quadrates), each of which must be sampled separately. The samples then can be mixed and homogenized. An aliquot drawn from this homogenous sample can be treated as representative sample of that area.

Scrap away surface liter; obtain a uniform thick slice of soil from the surface to the plough depth from each place. V-shaped cut is made with a spade obtain a uniformly thick slice of soil of the desired depth from each place. The sample may be collected on the blade of the spade and put in a clean bucket. In this way collect samples from all the spots marked for one sampling unit. In case of hard soil, samples are taken with the help of auger from the desired depth and collected in the bucket. Pour the soil from the bucket on a piece of clean paper or cloth and mix thoroughly. Spread the soil evenly and draw about 1kg sample. Reject rest of the soil. Put the soil sample in a polythene bag. Each bag should be properly marked to identify the sample. The bag used for sampling must always be clean and free from any contamination. Write the details of the sample in the information sheet.

(b) Sampling of soil in lab:

(Mixing and Preparation of Composite Samples)

The organic matter, like tree roots and pieces of bark should be removed from the sample. Similarity, matter other than soil, like shells are separated from the main soil sample.

- A sample collected from the sampling location is mixed by rolling or turning as follows: opposite corners of the cloth or gunny bag on which the sample is collected are held firmly.
- One corner is then pulled diagonally across the sample slowly so that soil rolls over the cloth towards the opposite corner.
- Then the opposite corner of the cloth is pulled back over the soil to roll it back.
- The process is repeated using the other corners of the cloth, and the entire procedure repeated 5-10 times to ensure a through mixture.
- The mixed sample is then coned in the center of the cloth, flattened, and divided into two equal parts with a flat metal sheet or spatula.
- Each half portion is again divided into half, making a total of four quarters in separate piles. Two diagonally opposite quarters are then discarded quantitatively and the remaining two mixed and preserved as the resulting composite sample.

SAMPLE PRESERVATION, HANDLING AND STORAGE

Chemical preservation of solids is not generally recommended.

Samples should, however, be cooled and protected from sunlight to minimize any potential reaction.

The collected sample should be kept in the shade to avoid fast drying and associated moisture loss.

PRECAUTIONS

- Do not sample unusual area like unevenly fertilized, marshy, old path, old channel, old bunds, area near the tree, and site of previous compost piles and other unrepresentative sites.
- Samples from the border area (about 50 cm) should be avoided.
- Avoid any type of contamination at all stages.
- Before putting soil samples in bags, they should be examined for cleanliness as well as for strength.
- Information sheet should be clearly written.

DETERMINATION OF PH

PRINCIPLE

The pH value which is a measure of the hydrogen (or hydroxyl) ion activity of the soil-water system indicates whether the soil is acidic, neutral or alkaline in reaction.

$pH = -\log [H^+]$

Apparatus

- pH meter
- Beaker

Reagents

(a) Deionized water

(b) pH - 7.0 buffer solution

(c) pH - 4.0 buffer solution

(d) pH - 9.18 buffer solution

PROCEDURE

1. Take 30 g of air-dried soil in a beaker.
2. Add 75 ml distilled water. Stir for a few seconds. Cover the beaker with a cover glass and allow standing for one hour.
3. Calibrate the pH meter using pH buffers. After washing the electrode with distilled water, immerse the electrode in the soil suspension.
4. The electrode is moved a little to ensure removal of water film around it and pH reading is again taken when it is constant.
5. Record the pH value.

CONDUCTIVITY

PRINCIPLE

Since ions are the carrier of electricity, the electrical conductivity (EC) of soil-water system rises according to the content of soluble salts in the soil giving rise to more of ions pairs on dissociation as it happens in case of a dilute solution. Thus the measurement of EC can be directly related to the soluble salts concentration of the soil at any particular temperature.

Apparatus

- Conductivity meter
- Beaker
- Thermometer 0 - 50°C

Reagents

Standard KCl (0.01 M): Dissolve 0.7456 g dry KCl in 1 liter of distilled water. This solution has an electrical conductivity of 1412 µS/cm at 25°C.

PROCEDURE

1. Take 20 g of air-dried soil in a conical flask/beaker.
2. Add 40ml distilled water.

3. Shake it for 30 min on the mechanical shaker.
4. Calibrate the conductivity meter using the standard 0.01M KCl solution.
5. Immerse the conductivity cell in the solution and measure conductivity as per the procedure given in the instrument manual.

MOISTURE CONTENT

PRINCIPLE

The moisture content in a solid sample is determined by drying a known quantity of sample in a Hot air Oven at 110°C ± 5°C and estimating the loss of weight.

APPARATUS

- Air-tight container
- Balance
- Desiccators

PROCEDURE

- Dry a clean and empty container with lid separately in a Hot Air Oven.
- Replace the lid and remove the container. Cool it in desiccators and weigh accurately.
- Take the required quantity of the soil sample in the container. Close lid and weigh. Remove the lid and keep it in the oven maintained at 110°C ± 5°C for about 24 hours.
- Replace the lid on the container, cool it in desiccators and record the final mass of the container with lid with dried soil sample.

CALCULATION

$$\text{Moisture (\%)} = \frac{(W2-W3)}{(W3-W1)} x\ 100$$

Where:

W2 = wt. of container with lid with wet soil in g

W3 = wt. of container with lid with dry soil in g

W1 = wt. of container with lid in g

ORGANIC CARBON AND ORGANIC MATTER

PRINCIPLE

Organic matter is oxidized with chromic acid (potassium dichromate + sulphuric acid). In the titration method, the unconsumed potassium dichromate is back-titrated against ferrous ammonium sulphate. Carbon in the sample is oxidized as follows:

$2H_2Cr_2O_7 + 3C + 6H_2SO_4 = 3\,Cr_2\,(SO_4)_3 + 8H_2O + 3CO_2$

Thus, $2H_2Cr_2O_7$ or $2K_2Cr_2O_{7a} \equiv 3C$

Or 588g of $K_2Cr_2O_7 \equiv$ 36g of C

Or 12 litres of 1N $K_2Cr_2O_7 \equiv$ 36 g of C

Or 1ml of 1N $K_2Cr_2O_7 \equiv$ 0.003 g of C

The excess Chromic acid left unutilized by the organic matter is back titrated with standard Ferrous Ammonium Sulphate, $Fe\,(NH_4)_2(SO_4)_2.6H_2O$ (1.0N) solution using Diphenylamine indicator.

Apparatus

- Analytical balance
- Conical flask (500 ml)
- Pipette (10 ml)
- Burette (50 ml)
- Measuring Cylinder (50 & 250 ml)

Reagents

- **Potassium dichromate (1N)**
  - Dissolve 49.035 g of dried potassium dichromate ($K_2Cr_2O_7$) in distilled water and make up to 1 liter.
- **Sulphuric acid (Conc.)**
- **Diphenylamine Indicator**
  - Dissolve 0.5 gm of the dye in a mixture of 20ml of distilled water and 100 ml of conc. Sulphuric acid.

- **Ferrous ammonium sulphate (0.5 N)**
  - Dissolve 196g of Fe $(NH_4)_2$ $(SO_4)_2.6H_2O$ in distilled water, add 20 ml of conc. H_2SO_4 and make volume to one litre.
- **Orthophosphoric acid (85%)**

PROCEDURE

- Take 1g or suitable quantity of oven dried (105°C) sample thoroughly ground and sieved through 0.2 mm sieve.
- Transfer the weighed sample to a 500-ml dry conical flask and add 10 ml of 1N $K_2Cr_2O_7$ solution.
- Then add 20 ml. Conc. H_2SO_4 and mix gently by rotation to ensure complete contact. Allow the mixture to stand for 30 minutes.
- Add 200 ml. distilled water, 10 ml of H_3PO_4 (85%) and 1 ml of Diphenylamine indicator. Titrate the solution with 0.5N Fe $(NH_4)_2$ $(SO_4)_2.6H_2O$ solution. Titrate the contents until green color starts appearing.
- Keep a blank titration without sample and follow the same procedure.

CALCULATION

$$\text{Organic Carbon (\%) in soil} = \frac{10(B-S)}{B} \times 0.003 \times \frac{100}{wt\ of\ sample\ (g)}$$

Where

B and S stand for the titre values (ml) of blank and sample, respectively.

The value of % Carbon can be expressed as % Organic Matter by multiplying % Carbon with the factor 1.724 as follows:

% Organic Matter = % C × 1.724

SODIUM

PRINCIPLE

Known amount of soil is leached with 1 N ammonium acetate of pH 7.0 and sodium is determined using flame photometer.

Apparatus

- Flame photometer
- Shaker
- 250 ml conical flask
- Funnel

Reagents

- **Ammonium acetate 1N, pH 7.0**

  Dissolve 77.08 g of ammonium acetate in 1 liter of distilled water. Adjust pH at 7.0 using either NH_4OH or glacial acetic acid.

- **Standard Na solution 1000 mg/l or CRM Na std**

  Take 2.542 g NaCl (dried at 110°C) and dissolve in 1 L.

PROCEDURE

- 5 g air-dried soil is shaken with 100ml of neutral 1N ammonium acetate. Shake the contents for 30 minutes and filter through Whattman No. 40. The extract is determined for sodium by Flame photometer.

CALCULATIONS

$$\text{Available Sodium mg of Na/kg soil} = \frac{A \times V}{W}$$

Where:

A = Na content of soil extract from flame photometer

V = vol. of soil extract, ml

W = wt. of air dry sample taken for extraction in g

POTASSIUM

PRINCIPLE

Known amount of soil is leached with 1 N ammonium acetate of pH 7.0 and potassium is determined using flame photometer.

Apparatus

- Flame photometer
- Shaker

- 250 ml conical flask
- Funnel

Reagents

- **Ammonium acetate 1N, pH 7.0**

  Dissolve 77.08 g of ammonium acetate in 1 liter of distilled water. Adjust pH at 7.0 using either NH_4OH or glacial acetic acid.
- **Standard K solution 1000 mg/l**

  Dissolve 0.9533 g of dried KCl in 500ml.

PROCEDURE

- 5 g air-dried soil is shaken with 100ml of neutral 1N ammonium acetate. Shake the contents for 30 minutes and filter through Whattman No. 40. Potassium concentration in the extract is determined by Flame photometer.

CALCULATIONS

$$\text{Available potassium mg of K/kg soil} = \frac{A \times V}{W}$$

Where:

A= K content of soil extract from flame photometer, mg/l

V= vol. of soil extract, ml

W= wt. of air dry sample taken for extraction in g.

CALCIUM AND MAGNESIUM

PRINCIPLE

Calcium and magnesium can be determined in Ammonium acetate extracts of soil by titration with EDTA. Both Ca and Mg may be titrated at pH 10 using Erichrome Black T as an indicator. Magnesium for ms insoluble Mg $(OH)_2$ at pH 12 or higher if NH_4 salts are present, there allowing Ca to be titrated using muroxide or calgon as an indicator.

Reagents

- **Ammonium chloride-ammonium hydroxide buffer solution:** Dissolve 67.5 g NH_4Cl in 570 ml of conc.NH_4OH and make to 1L.

- **Erichrome black T indicator:** Dissolve 0.5g of indicator in 100g NaCl.
- **Muroxide (ammonium purpurate) indicator:** Mix 0.2 g of ammonium purpurate and 100g of sodium chloride and grind thoroughly too fine powder.
- **Sodium hydroxide solution (4N):** Dissolve 160 g 0f NaOH in 1L of distilled water.
- **Standard Calcium Solution:** Weigh accurately 1 g AR grade $CaCO_3$ (dried at 180°C for 1h before weighing) and dissolved in a minimum of 0.2 N HCl and dilute to 1L.
- **Standard EDTA solution (0.01M):** Dissolve 3.723 g EDTA sodium salt and dilute to 1L.

PROCEDURE

- 5 g air-dried soil is shaken with 100ml of neutral 1N ammonium acetate. Shake the contents for 30 minutes and filter through Whatman No. 40.

Estimation of total Ca and Mg:

- Take 5-25 mL of aliquot in a conical flask.
- Next add 2 mL of buffer solution.
- Add a pinch of Erichrome black T indicator.
- The contents are titrated with standard EDTA solution to a pure blue end point.

Estimation of Ca:

- 5-25 mL of aliquot is taken in a 100 mL of conical flask; and 5 mL of 4N NaOH is added to precipitated Magnesium as $Mg(OH)_2$.
- Next, add a pinch of Muroxide indicator.
- The contents are titrated against 0.01N EDTA to an orange red to purple or violet colour.

CALCULATION

$$\text{Calcium, mg of Ca/kg soil} = \frac{\text{R2} \times \text{M} \times 40.08 \times 100 \times 1000}{wt \times v}$$

Where R_1 = ml of EDTA required for titration
M = Molarity of EDTA
Wt. = wt of soil taken in g
V= vol of aliquot taken, ml

Calculation of Total Ca and Mg

$$(Ca+Mg), mg/kg \text{ soil} = \frac{R2 \times M \times 100 \times 100 \times 1000}{wt \times v}$$

$$\text{Magnesium, mg of mg/kg soil} = \frac{(R2-R1) \times M \times 24.3 \times 100 \times 1000}{wt \times V}$$

AVAILABLE NITROGEN

PRINCIPLE

Ammonium salts and nitrate constitute soil available nitrogen.

Soil sample is extracted by shaking with KCl & NO_3-N and NH_3-N is estimated after reduction of nitrate to ammonia followed by its measurement by distillation method.

Apparatus

- Steam distillation equipment
- 250 ml conical flask
- Funnel
- Burette & pipette
- Measuring Cylinder (100 ml)
- Shaker

Reagents

- **1 N KCl:** Dissolved 74.55g KCl in 1 lit of distilled water.
- **Phenophthalein Indicator**
- **Mixed indicator:**

  Dissolved 500 mg bromocresol green & 100 mg methyl red in 100 ml of 95% ethanol. Adjust pH to 4.5 using NaOH/HCl.

- **Boric acid 2%:**
  Dissolve 20 gm H_3BO_3 in 1 lit of distilled water containing 10 ml mixed indicator.
- **Devarda alloy powder**
- **MgO**
- N/50 H_2SO_4

PROCEDURE

Extraction

1. Take 20 gm air dried soil sample in 250 ml conical flask and add 40 ml 1 N KCl.
2. Shake the content for 60 minute using wrist shaker and filter using Whatman No. 40 filter paper.

Distillation

1. NH_4-N: Transfer 20 ml of extract into distillation flask; add 10 ml of distilled water, few drops of phenolphthalein indicator and one spoonful of MgO. Distill ammonia and collect the distillate into 50 ml 2% boric acid solution. Titrate the borate solution with N/ 50 H_2SO_4.
2. NO_3-N: Add a spoonful of Devarda alloy to the distillation flask and continue distillation. Nitrates are reduced to ammonia. Collect the distillate into 50 ml 2% boric acid solution and determine the ammonia by titration with N/50 H_2SO_4.

CALCULATION

$$NH_4\text{-N, mg/100 g Soil} = \frac{N \times R \times 14 \times 100}{10}$$

$$NO_3\text{- N, mg/100 g Soil} = \frac{N \times R \times 14 \times 100}{10}$$

Where

N = normality of H_2SO_4

R = ml H_2SO_4, required for sample titration

20 ml extract = 10 g soil

AVAILABLE PHOSPHOROUS

PRINCIPLE

Soil available phosphorous, which can be correlated with the response of crop to phosphate fertilizer, is extracted with alkaline $NaHCO_3$ (Olsen method).

Apparatus

- Spectrophotometer
- Analytical balance-Shaker
- Conical flask (50 ml)
- Volumetric flask (50,250, and 1000 ml)
- Funnel
- Pipette
- Measuring cylinder (100 ml)

Reagents

(a) **0.5 M $NaHCO_3$:** Dissolve 42 g $NaHCO_3$ in 1 liter of distilled water and adjust pH to 8.5 with dilute NaOH.

(b) Phosphate free activated charcoal

(c) **Chloromolybdic acid 1.5%:** Dissolve 15 g ammonium Molybdate $(NH_4)6\ MO_7O_{24}$. $4H_2O$ in 300 ml hot distilled water. Cool the solution and add 350 ml 10 NHCl and dilute to 1 liter. This, solution is stable for 60 days.

(d) **Chlorostannous acid reductant:** Dissolve 10 g $SnCl_2.2H_2O$ in 25 ml HCl. Warm necessary. This concentrated solution can be stored in refrigerator. Dilute 1 ml conc. Solution to 132 ml with distilled water and use for estimation. Dilute solution is unstable and thus needs to be prepared freshly.

(e) 4N NH_4OH

(f) 4N HCl

(g) **2, 4-dinitrophenol indicator:** Dissolve 250 mg 2, 4-dinitrophenol in 100 distilled water.

(h) **Standard phosphate solution 50 ppm of P:** Weigh 0.2195 g KH_2PO4 previously dried at 40°C and dissolve in distilled water. Add 25 ml 7N H_2SO_4 and make the volume to 1 liter. Dilute solution (2ppm): Dilute 10 ml of the 50 ppm stock solution to 250 ml.

PROCEDURE

Extraction

1. Shake 5 g air-dried soil with 100 ml 0.5 M $NaHCO_3$ and 1 teaspoon of activated charcoal in 250 ml conical flask for 30 minutes.
2. Filter the solution using Whatman No. 40. If filtrate is not clear, add more activated. Charcoal, shake and filter again.

Estimation

1. Pipette a 10 ml clear extract into 50 ml volumetric flask.
2. Add 2-3 drops of 2,4-dinitrophenol indicator and adjust pH to 3 with 4N NH_4OH or 4N HCl (indicator turns yellow when pH approaches 3).
3. Add 10 ml Chloromolybdic acid to the aliquot and allow the flask to stand quietly for a few minutes and dilute the solution to 40 ml with distilled water.
4. Then add 1 ml dilute stannous chloride solution, mix the contents immediately and dilute to 50 ml.
5. Read the absorbance/transmission at 660 mμ after 10 minutes.
6. Colour stability is for 20 minutes only.

Standard Curve

(a) Take 1.0, 2.5, 5.0, 10.0, 15.0 and 20 ml of 2 ppm stock solution in 50 ml volumetric flask.

(b) Add 10 ml 0.5 M $NaHCO_3$ solution, 2 to 3 drops 2,4-dinitrophenol and just the pH to 3.0 using 4N HCl or 4N NH_4OH.

(c) Then add 10 ml Chloromolybdic acid and allow the flask to stand for a few minutes and dilute the solution to 40 ml.

(d) Add 1 ml stannous chloride and dilute the solution to 50 ml. Read the absorbance after 10 minutes at 660 mμ.

CALCULATION

P, mg/kg soil = p*v* 100/w

Where

P = mg of phosphorous in soil

V = vol. of extracting solution

W = wt. of soil taken

CATION EXCHANGE CAPACITY

PRINCIPLE

The determination of Cation Exchange Capacity (CEC) of soil involves measuring the total quantity of negative charges per unit weight of soil. It is usually measured by leaching the soil with 1 N salt solution, preferably using ammonium acetate, buffered at a neutral pH and then washing out the excess salt with an electrolyte free solvent. The buffer (1 N ammonium acetate) function is followed by washing with a saturated metallic Cation, KCl solution. The ammonia leached out after filtering is distilled, estimated and CEC of soil is determined.

Apparatus

- Buchner Funnel
- Suction flask
- Conical flask (250 ml)
- Distillation assembly
- Vacuum pump. - Burette and pipette

Reagents

(a) **Ammonium acetate, I N:** Dissolve 77.08 g ammonium acetate (NH_4OAc) in 1 liter of distilled water and adjust to pH 7.0.

(b) **Isopropyl alcohol:** 99 %

(c) **Potassium Chloride, 10%:** Dissolve 100 g KCl in 900 ml distilled water, adjust the pH to 2.5 with HCl and dilute to 1 liter.

(d) **Sulphuric acid, 1 N:** Slowly and while stirring, add 28 mL of concentrated sulphuric acid (H_2SO_4) to distilled water and dilute of 1 liter.

(e) **Standard Sulphuric acid solution, 0.02 N:** Dilute 20 ml volume of 1 N. H_2SO_4 to 1000 ml with distilled water. Standardize it against 0.02 N sodium carbonate Solution using methyl orange as indicator. At the end point a faint orange color will appear.

(f) **Ammonium chloride Salt.**

(g) **Mixed indicator:** Dissolve 500 mg bromocresol green and 100 mg methyl red in 100 ml of 95% ethanol. Adjust pH to 4.5 using NaOH/HCl.

(h) **Boric acid, 4%:** Dissolve 40 g H_3BO_3 in 1 liter of distilled water containing 10 ml Mixed indicator.

(i) **Sodium hydroxide, 40%:** Dissolve 400 g NaOH in 1 liter of distilled/rater.

PROCEDURE

1. Take 50 g air dried soil sample in 250 ml conical flask containing 100 ml of 1 N NH_4OAc and shake for 1 hr. and then allow to stand overnight.
2. Transfer the contents to Buchner funnel fitted with Whatman No. 42 filter paper and leach the soil with 400 ml of NH_4OAc using about 80-100 ml of NH_4OAc at a time.
3. Adjust the leaching rate in such a *way* that leaching will take at least 1-2 hrs.
4. Preserve the leach ate for estimation of exchangeable Cation if necessary.
5. Add a pinch of ammonium Chloride salt to soil and wash the soil with isopropyl alcohol till free of chloride (about 200-250 m1 of isopropy1 alcohol is required).
6. Care should be taken that at this stage soil should not dry, otherwise ammonia will be lost.
7. Then leach the soil with 450 m1 of 10% KCl solution of pH 2.5 and collect the Leachate in a flask. Transfer the extract to volumetric flask and make up to 500 ml.

8. Transfer 25 to 50 ml of the above extract into a distillation flask; add few drops of phenolphthalein indicator and 40% NaOH till the contents are alkaline.
9. Distill for ammonia and collect the distillate in 4% boric acid.
10. Titrate the absorbed ammonia with 0.02N H_2SO_4.

CALCULATION

CEC, meq/100g = N*R*final vol. of leachate soil/vol of leachate soil taken *100/s.wt

Where

N = normality of H_2SO_4

R = ml. of H_2SO_4 required for titration

BULK DENSITY

PRINCIPLE

Bulk density of the soil is the dry weight of a unit volume of it. It is expressed as g/cm^3.

Apparatus

- Measuring Cylinder
- Oven
- Chemical Balance

METHOD

Dry the sample in an over at 105° C until constant weight. Now put a little dried soil in a measuring cylinder and record the volume. Now find out the weight of this volume of soil in a chemical balance.

CALCULATIONS

$$\text{Bulk Density} = \frac{\text{Weight of dry soil (g)}}{\text{Volume of dry soil (cm}^3\text{)}} = \text{g/cm}^3$$

W1 = Weight of empty cylinder in g.

W2 = Weight of cylinder + soil (in gm).

V = Volume of soil in cm^3

WATER HOLDING CAPACITY

PRINCIPLE

When soil is soaked with water, water fills all the pores between the particles of soil and no air space exists as in the case of aquatic sediments. Such a soil is said to be at its maximum water holding capacity or saturation.

Apparatus

- Filter Paper
- Petri Dish
- Oven
- Balance

Method

Take a funnel and plug its passage by cotton. Fill it 1/3 with the sample. Add water drop wise into it till the sample becomes saturated by water (drop of water starts pouring out of the funnel).

Weight the oven dried empty Petri dish. Take 4-5g of the water saturated soil sample into it and weigh. Then put it into the oven at 105°C for 1-2 hour. Cool into the desiccators and weight.

CALCULATIONS

$$\text{Water Holding Capacity (\% by mass)} = \frac{(W2-W3)}{(W2-W1)} \times 100$$

Where

W2 = Weight of Petri dish filled with water saturated soil

W3 = Weight of Petri dish + sample after oven drying at 105°C.

W1 = Weight of empty petri dish

CHLORIDE

PRINCIPLE

The conc. of chloride is determined by back titration with potassium thiocyanate using ferric ammonium sulphate indicator.

Reagents

- **Silver nitrate solution (0.1N):** Dry 5g of $AgNO_3$ for 2 hours at100°C and allow to cool. Accurately weigh about 4.25 g of solid $AgNO_3$ and dissolve it in 250 ml of distilled water in a conical flask. Store the solution in a brown bottle.
- **Potassium thiocyanate solution (0.1N):** Weigh 2.43 g of solid KSCN and dissolve it in 250ml of distilled water in a volumetric flask.
- **Potassium Permanganate Solution (5%):** Add 1.5 g $KMnO_4$ to 3oo ml distilled water.
- **Ferric Ammonium Sulfate Indicator:** Add8 g to 20 ml of distilled water and add a few drops of conc. Nitric acid.
- **Conc. Nitric Acid**

PROCEDURE

- Take 5g of air dried soil in beaker and digest with dilute HNO_3 and volume make up to 250 ml with distilled water.
- Take 50 ml of aliquot and add 10 ml of 0.1N $AgNO_3$ and titrate against 0.1N Potassium thiocyanate using ferric ammonium sulfate indicator until color changes from yellow to brick red. Run a blank without soil extract.

CALCULATION

$$\text{Cl (\% by mass)} = \frac{(B-S)\times N\times 35.45\times 250\times 100}{1000\times 50\times \textit{sample wt taken}}$$

Where, B=vol. of KCNS consumed for blank

S= vol. of KCNS consumed for sample

N = Normality of $AgNO_3$

TURBIDIMETRIC METHOD

REAGENTS

- **Morgan's Extraction Solution:** 100 g of sodium acetate and 30 ml of 99.5% acetic acid dissolved and mixed in 500 ml of water and the volume made to 1 litre.

- **25% Gum Acacia:** 25 g of chemically pure gum acacia is dissolved in 100 ml of hot water and the hot solution filtered through Whatman No. 42 filter paper.
- **Barium Chloride Crystals**
- **Stock Solution:** Dissolve 0.888g anhydrous sodium sulphate/ alcoholic (N) ammonium chloride (NH_4Cl). This gives a conc. of 0.60 mg of SO_4/ml.
- **Working Std.:** Dilute 0.60 mg SO_4/ml stock solution with alcoholic (N) ammonium chloride to give 0.06 mg SO_4/ ml. Take 2, 4, 6,8,10 ml of this to give a range of 0.12-0.60 mg of SO_4.

PROCEDURE

- Weigh 20 g air-dry soil in a 250 ml conical flask. Add 100 ml of Morgan's extraction solution. Shake the suspension for one-half hour and filter through Whatmans No. 42 filter. Take 10 ml aliquot and add 1 g of barium chloride crystals.
- Add 1 or 2 ml of 25% gum acacia A suitable aliquot of the extract is taken in a 25 ml volumetric flask to which 2.5 ml of 25% nitric acid and 2 ml of acetic-phosphoric acid are added and diluted to about 22 ml.
- The flask is stoppered and shaken. Then add 0.5 ml of Barium Sulphate seed suspension and 0.2 g of Barium Chloride crystals are added successively.
- Allowing for another 5 minutes, 1 ml of gum acacia-acetic acid solution is put in and diluted to volume and inverted 3 times.
- Then reading taken at 420 mμ.

CALCULATION

Sulphate, (mg/kg) = Abs.*factor*1000*250/ (10*s.wt)

BORON

PRINCIPLE

Boron in soil extracts is measured calorimetrically using azomethine-H.

APPARATUS

- Erlenmeyer flasks 50 ml (Pyrex), pre-treated with concentrated HCL for one week.
- Spectrophotometer or colorimeter, 420-nm wavelength.
- Polypropylene test tubes, 10-ml capacity

REAGENTS

- **Buffer solution:** Dissolve 250 g ammonium acetate (NH_4OAc), and 15 g ethylene-diamine-tetra-acetic acid, disodium salt (EDTA disodium) in 400 ml dilute water. Slowly add 125 ml glacial acetic acid (CH_3COOH), and mix well.
- **Azomethine-H Solution ($C_{17}H_{12}NNa\ O_8S_2$):** Dissolve 0.45 g azomethine-H in 100 ml 1% L-ascorbic acid solution. Fresh reagent should be prepared weekly and stored in a refrigerator.
- **Activated Charcoal (Boron-free)**

  This is prepared by giving repeated washings (8-9 times) of dilute water (boiling Charcoal with water in 1:5 ratio), and subsequent filtering. Boron in the filtrate is checked by azomethine–H color development. Continue washing until it is B free.
- **Standard Stock Solution:**
  - *(i)* Dissolve 0.114 g boric acid (H_3BO_3) in dilute water, and bring to 1-litre volume with dilute water. This solution contains 20 ppm B (Stock Solution).
  - *(ii)* Prepare a series of Standard Solutions from the Stock Solutions as follows:
  - *(iii)* Dilute 2.5, 5.0, 7.5, 10.0, 12.5, and 15.0 ml Stock Solution to 100 ml final volume by adding dilute water. These solutions contain 0.5, 1.0, 1.5, 2.0, 2.5, and 3.0 ppm, respectively.
- **Hydrochloric Acid (HCL), 0.05 N:**

  Dilute 4.14 ml concentrated hydrochloric acid (37%, sp. gr. 1.19) in dilute water, mix well, and bring to 1-litre volume with dilute water.

PROCEDURE

(a) Extraction

- Weigh 10 gm air-dry soil (2 mm) into a polypropylene tube.
- Add about 0.2 gm activated charcoal (Boron-free).
- Add 20 ml 0.05 N Hydrochloric acid solution.
- Shake for 5 minutes, and then filter.

(b) Measurement (by Azomethine –H Method)

- Pipette 1 ml of aliquot of the extract into a 10 ml polypropylene tube.
- Add 2 ml buffer solution.
- Add 2 ml azomethine-H solution, and mix well.
- Prepare a Standard curve as follows:
  (a) Pipette 1 ml of each standard (0.5-3.0 ppm), and proceed as for the samples.
  (b) Also make a blank with 1 ml dilute water, and proceed as for the samples.
  (c) Read the absorbance of blank, standards, and samples after 30 minutes at 420 nm wavelength.
  (d) Prepare a Calibration curve for standards, plotting absorbance against the respective.
  (e) Boron concentrations.
- Read Boron concentration in the unknown samples from the calibration curve.

CALCULATION

Boron in (ppm) = Boron in ppm from calibration curve) $\times A/W$

Where

A = Total volume of the extract (ml)

W = Weight of air-dry soil (g).

PERMEABILITY (CONSTANT HEAD METHOD)

PRINCIPLE

Rate of movement of water through the soil media is measured by Constant Head Method using soil permeability test apparatus.

Apparatus

- Soil core sampler
- Funnel
- Beaker
- Wire mesh/muslin cloth
- Constant head device
- Thermometer

PROCEDURE

(a) Preparation of remolded soil specimen:

1. Weight the required quantity of oven dried soil sample. Evenly sprinkle the calculated quantity of water corresponding to the OMC. Mix the soil sample thoroughly.
2. Clean the mould and apply a small portion of grease inside the mould and around the porous stones in the base plate. Keep the apparatus on solid base.
3. The soil sample is placed inside the mould, and is compacted by the standard proctor compaction tools, to achieve a dry density equal to the pre-determined MDD. Weight the mould along with the compacted soil.
4. Saturate the porous stones. Place the filter papers on both ends of the soil specimen in the mould. Attach the mould with the drainage base and cap having saturated porous stones.

(b) Saturation of soil Specimen:

1. Connect the water reservoir to the outlet at the bottom and allow the water to flow in the soil. Wait till the water has been able to travel up and saturate the sample. Allow about 1cm depth of free water to.

2. Collect on the top of the sample.
3. Fill the remaining portion of cylinder with de-aired water without disturbing the surface of soil.
4. Fix the cover plate over the collar and tighten the nuts in the rods.

(c) **Constant Head Test:**

1. Place the mould assembly in the bottom tank and fill the bottom tank with water up to the outlet.
2. Connect the outlet tube with constant head tank to the inlet nozzle of the permeameter, after removing the air in flexible rubber tubing connecting the tube.
3. Adjust the hydraulic head by either adjusting the relative height of the permeameter mould and constant head tank or by rising or lowering the air intake tube with in the head tank.
4. Start the stop watch and at the same time put a bucket under the outlet of the bottom tank, run the test for same convenient time interval and measure.
5. Repeat the test twice more, under the same head and for the same time interval.

PRECAUTIONS

1. All possible leakage of joint must be eliminated.
2. Porous stones must be saturated before being put to use.
3. De-aired and distilled water should be used to prevent choking of flowing water.
4. Soil sample must be carefully saturated before taking the observations.
5. Use of high head, which result in turbulent flows, should be avoided.

CALCULATION

K=Q * 1/tiA (I = (hydraulic gradients) $\frac{h}{L}$

$$=\frac{Q}{t}\frac{L}{h}\frac{1}{A}$$

Where,

K = Coefficient of permeability at T °C (cm/sec).

L = Length of soil specimen (cm)

A = Total cross-sectional area of soil sample

Q = Quantity of water collected in measuring jar

t = Total time required for collecting Q quantity of water.

h = Difference in the water levels of the overhead and bottom tank.

TOTAL KJELDAHL NITROGEN (T.K.N)

PRINCIPLE

Total Kjeldahl Nitrogen is the sum of ammonical nitrogen and Organic nitrogen present in sample. It does not include nitrite nitrogen and nitrate nitrogen. In the presence of sulphuric acid, potassium sulphate and cupric sulphate (catalysts), the nitrogen of organic matter as well as free ammonia is converted to ammonium sulphate on digestion at 360-410°C.

Apparatus

- Kjeldahl flask, 500 ml capacity.
- Heating device
- Fume hood or scrubber unit
- Kjeldahl Distillation unit
- Measuring Cylinder (100 ml)
- Shaker

Reagents

- Sulphuric acid (conc.)
- Potassium sulphate – Copper sulphate mixture (10:1 ratio)
- **Phenolphthalein Indicator:**

  Dissolve 0.5 gm of phenolphthalein in 50ml ethyl or isopropyl alcohol and 50ml distilled water.

- **Mixed indicator:**

  Dissolved 500 mg bromocresol green & 100 mg methyl red in 100 ml of 95% ethanol. Adjust pH to 4.5 using NaOH/HCl.

- **Sodium Hydroxide solution (50%)**

  Dissolve 50 gm NaOH in 100 ml.distilled water.

- **Boric acid 2%:**

  Dissolve 20 gm H_3BO_3 in 1 lit of distilled water containing 10 ml mixed indicator.

- **Standard Sulphuric acid solution(0.02N)**

  Dilute 20 ml of 1N sulphuric acid to 1000 ml with distilled water .standardized it against 0.02N sodium carbonate solution (1.06 gm of sodium carbonate in 1 liter) using methyl red indicator. A faint orange colour will appear at the end point.

PROCEDURE

Digestion

1. Take 2.0 gm or suitable quantity of oven dried (105°C) sample thoroughly ground and sieved though 0.2 mm sieve in a kjeldahl digestion flask.
2. Add 10 gm potassium sulphate and 1.0 gm copper sulphate and add 35 ml of conc. Sulphuric acid.
3. Heat initially at low temperature for first 10 to 30 min. until frothing stops and then raise the temperature gradually to 360-410 °C. Continue the digestion until the contents become light yellow colour.

Distillation

1. Cool the digested sample and add 50 ml of distilled water. Mix thoroughly, let it stand for few minutes and transfer the content in 1 liter distillation flask.
2. Carry out 4-5 washings with 50 ml of distilled water and transfer the content of every washing into the same distillation flask making the final volume of about 300 ml.

3. The solution is made alkaline (Ph-11) with 50% sodium hydroxide solution using phenolphthalein indicator. Immediately attach the distillation flask to the distillation unit.
4. Start distillation after immersing the tip of the condenser in 50 ml boric acid solution with mixed indicator in a conical flask. Collect about 150 ml of the distillate.

Titration

1. Titrate the boric acid solution against the standardized sulphuric acid (0.02N)
2. The end point is the appearance of purple colour.
3. Carry out blank titration similarly using distilled water as blank.

CALCULATION

$$\textbf{TKN mg/kg} = \frac{\textbf{(S-B)}* \text{N}*14*1000}{\text{Wt. of sample}}$$

N = normality of H_2SO_4

S = ml H_2SO_4, required for sample titration

B = ml H_2SO_4, required for blank titration

SODIUM ADSORPTION RATIO

PRINCIPLE

- SAR is defined as The Square Root of Ratio of The Sodium (Na) to Calcium Plus Magnesium (Ca + Mg)
- Sodium Adsorption ratio is calculated by Using The Formula

$$SAR = \frac{[Na^{+}]}{\sqrt{\frac{1}{2}([Ca^{2+}] + [Mg^{2+}])}}$$

Where:

Na = sodium content in meq/kg

Ca = Calcium content in meq/kg

Mg = magnesium content in meq/kg

POROSITY

PRINCIPLE

Soil porosity (amount of pore space) - Soil porosity is the ratio of the volume of soil pores to the total soil volume.

Apparatus

- Measuring Cylinder
- Oven
- Chemical Balance
- Pycnometer- Glass Bottle of 50 ml capacity
- Funnel
- Spoon
- Hexane

METHOD

Bulk Density

Dry the sample in an oven at 105° C until constant weight. Now put a little dried soil in a measuring cylinder and record the volume. Now find out the weight of this volume of soil in a chemical balance.

$$\text{Bulk Density} = \frac{\text{Volume of dry soil (cm}^3)}{\text{Weight of dry soil (g)}} = \text{g/cm}^3$$

W1 = Weight of empty watch glass in gm.

W2 = Weight of empty watch glass and soil in gm.

V = Volume of soil in cm^3

Standard Particle Density (SPD):

- Take a clean, dry 50 ml capacity pycnometer and Weigh the empty pycnometer and record the weight.
- Then take empty pycnometer and add 5 gm oven dried soil and record the weight.
- Fill the pycnometer with hexane up to the mark; clean the exterior surface of the pycnometer with a clean and dry cloth. Determine the weight of the pycnometer and content.

- Empty the pycnometer and clean it. Then fill it with hexane only (to the mark). Determine the weight of pycnometer and hexane.

  Calculation:

$$G = \frac{M_2 - M_1}{(M_2 - M_1) - (M_3 - M_4)}$$

Where

M1 = mass of empty Pycnometer,

M2 = mass of the Pycnometer with dry soil

M3 = mass of the Pycnometer and sample +hexane

M4 = mass of Pycnometer filled with hexane only.

G = Standard practical density

Calculation of porosity

Porosity = (SPD-BD)*100 /SPD

Metals (Fe, Pb, Cu, Ni, Cr, Mn, Zn, Cd)*

Take 1-2 g of sample to a digestion vessel. Add 10ml of 1:1 HNO_3 mix the slurry and cover with a watch glass. Heat the sample for 10-15 minutes. Add 5ml of conc. HNO_3. Repeat until digestion is completed. Conc. it to about 5ml. then cool it. Add some water and 3ml of 30% H_2O_2. Heat until effervescence subsides and cools the vessel. Continue to add 1ml 30% H_2O_2 with warming until the effervescence is minimal. (Do not add more than a total of 10ml 30% H_2O_2. Reduce volume to around 5ml by heating. Add 10ml conc. HCl and heat it again. Filter through Whatman no. 41 filter paper. Then make up the volume. Analyse the requisite metal by AAS.

Metal conc., mg/kg = conc. by AAS * make up volume/ sample weight

*By using AAS

REFERENCES

Soil Chemical Analysis by M.L. Jackson, Vohlard's method.

This method is based on Chapman, H.D., "Cation-exchange Capacity," pp. 891-900, in C.A. Black (ed.), Method of Soil Analysis, Part 2: Chemical and Microbiological Properties, Am. Soc. Agron., Madison, Wisconsin (1965).

This method is based on Chapman, H.D., "Cation-exchange Capacity," pp. 891-900, in C.A. Black (ed.), Method of Soil Analysis, Part 2: Chemical and Microbiological Properties, Am. Soc. Agron., Madison, Wisconsin (1965).

Walkley, A. and I.A. Black. 1934. An Examination of Degtjareff Method for Determining Soil Organic Matter and a Proposed Modification of the Chromic Acid Titration Method. Soil Sci. 37: 29-37.

Analysis of Plant Samples

RELATIVE WATER CONTENT

Relative water or moisture content is a devise for measuring the water status of a tissue in term of quantity of water and expressed as % of water content of fully turgid tissue.

PROCEDURE

1. Take plant leaf and cut it into small piece and weigh.
2. Then dip it into the water for 24 hrs and weigh again.
3. Then put the sample in oven at 100 °C for at least 5 hrs then dry weight was noted.

CALCULATION

% moisture content = (F-D/T-D) × 100

Where:

F = fresh weight of leaves

D = dry weight of leaves

T = Turgid weight of leaves

pH

pH is a measure of hydrogen ion activity and largely depends on the relative amounts of absorbed hydrogen ions and metallic ions.

pH = - log 10 (H^+)

or

pH = log 10 (1/H^+)

It is a very good measure of the intensity of acidity or alkalinity of the leaf wash extract and provides a good identification of the air pollution and its chemical nature. pH was measured electrometrically with pH meter. pH meter uses hydrogen sensitive electrode called indicator electrode and calomel reference electrode. The indicator electrode is generally made of highly sensitive and thin glass membrane.

PROCEDURE

1. 1 gm of leaf wash was taken in a beaker.
2. 50 ml of distilled water was added to it.
3. The pH meters electrode was immersed in the leaf wash extract and reading was taken.

PHOTOSYNTHETIC PIGMENTS; CHLOROPHYLL AND CAROTENOIDS

This method is widely used for the determination of photosynthetic pigments of green plants. A number of studies have shown that chlorophyll content can be used as an index of photosynthetic activity. In green plants, chlorophyll 'a' and chlorophyll 'b' are principal photosynthetic pigments. More the chlorophyll content, more the photosynthesis and more is productivity.

REAGENTS

1. 80% acetone
2. Magnesium Carbonate (blank solution)
3. Spectrophotometer
4. Motor and pistle

PROCEDURE

One gram of fresh leaves were taken and cut into small pieces (about 1 mm wide) with scissors, leaves were grinded in 20 ml of 80% acetone and filtered, transferred the homogenate to a Buchner funnel fitted with whatman No. 1 filter paper and filtered the extract.

Measure the optical density (absorbance) of the extract with the help of spectrophotometer. Measure optical density at 480 nm, 510 nm, 644 nm, 645 nm and 663 nm. These are positions in the spectrum where maximum absorption by chlorophyll *a* and *b* occur. The concentration of chlorophyll *a* and *b*, in mg/g of tissue, is calculated by the following formula:

Chlorophyll *a* (mg/g fresh weight) = $[12.7\ D_{663} - 0.094\ D_{645}]/(d \times 1000 \times W) \times V$

Chlorophyll *b* (mg/g fresh weight) = $[1.77\ D_{644} - 0.280\ .D_{663}/(d \times 1000 \times W) \times V$

Carotenoids (mg/g fresh weight) = $[7.6\ D_{480} - 1.49 D_{510}]/(d \times 1000 \times W) \times V$

Where:

V = volume of chlorophyll solution (extract) in acetone

d = the length of the light path (cm)

W = fresh weight (gm) of leaves.

ASCORBIC ACID

Ascorbic acid, a natural antioxidant in plants has been shown to play an important role in pollution tolerance.

REAGENTS

1. 4% oxalic Acid (40 gm oxalic acid +1 liter distilled water)
2. Dye Solution: 42 mg of sodium bicarbonate + 20 ml of distilled water, then dissolve 52 mg dichlorophenol indophenol and make up to 200 ml by adding distilled water.
3. Standard stock solution: 100 mg of ascorbic acid dissolve in 100 ml of 4% oxalic acid.

WORKING STANDARD

Make up 10 ml of stock solution to 100 ml by adding 4% oxalic Acid.

PROCEDURE

1. Take 5 ml of working standard in 100 ml of conical flask and add 10 ml of 4% oxalic acid. Titrate against the dye and note the point in appearance of pink color, which persists for a few minutes (V_1 ml).

2. Extract 1 gm of sample in 10 ml of 40% oxalic acid and filter, collect the filterate and make the volume up to 100 ml by adding 4% oxalic acid.
3. Pipette out 5 ml of the extract, add 10 ml of 4% oxalic acid and titrate against dye.

CALCULATION

Ascorbic acid mg/100 gm sample =

= (0.5mg/V_1ml) × (V_2 m1 /5m1) × (100m1/wt. of the sample) × 100

Where:

V_1 = Reading with standard

V_2 = Reading with extract

AIR POLLUTION TOLERANCE INDEX FOR PLANTS

To evaluate the tolerance level of plant species to air pollution, Singh and Rao (1983) used four leaf parameters to derive an empirical number indicating the Air Pollution Tolerance Index (APTI). APTI is thus calculated as follows:

APTI = [A (T+P)] + R/10

Where:

A = ascorbic acid content

T = total chlorophyll content

P = pH of the leaf extract

R = relative water content of leaf.

Protein and proline methods.

ESTIMATION OF PROTEIN BY LOWRY'S METHOD

PRINCIPLE

Lowry's assay for total protein estimation is one of the most commonly used colorimetric assays. It is sensitive, highly reproducible, inexpensive and easy to perform. It relies on the reaction of copper with protein, but the sample is also incubated with the Folin - Ciocaltaeu Reagent. Reduction of the Folin - Ciocaltaeu Reagent under alkaline conditions results in an intense blue colour (hetero polymolybdenum blue) product showing absorption maxima in the range of 650-750 nm based on the concentration of protein in the sample. This is the best method used for protein concentration in the range of 0.01-1 mg/mL.

REAGENTS

1. 2% Na_2CO_3 in 0.1 N NaOH
2. 1% NaK Tartrate in H_2O
3. 0.5% $CuSO_4.5\ H_2O$ in H_2O
4. Reagent I: 48 ml of reagent 1, 1 ml of reagent 2, 1 ml reagent 3
5. Reagent II: 1 part Folin-Phenol [2 N]: 1 part water
6. BSA Standard - 1 mg/ml

PROCEDURE

1. 0.2 ml of BSA working standard in 5 test tubes and make up to 1ml using distilled water.
2. The test tube with 1 ml distilled water serve as blank.
3. Add 4.5 ml of Reagent I and incubate for 10 minutes.
4. After incubation add 0.5 ml of reagent II and incubate for 30 minutes.
5. Measure the absorbance at 660 nm and plot the standard graph.
6. Estimate the amount of protein present in the given sample from the standard graph.

ESTIMATION OF PROLINE

PRINCIPLE

During selective extraction with aqueous sulphosalicylic acid, proteins are precipitated as a complex. Other interfering materials are also presumably removed by absorption to the protein-sulphosalicylic acid complex. The extracted proline is made to react with ninhydrin in acidic conditions (pH 1.0) to form the chlorophore (red color) and read at 520nm.

REAGENTS

1. Acid Ninhydrin
2. Warm 1.25g ninhydrin in 30mL glacial acetic acid and 20mL ^M phosphoric acid, with agitation until dissolved. Store at 4°C and use within 24h
3. 3% Aqueous Sulphosalicyclic Acid
4. Glacial Acetic Acid
5. Toluene
6. Proline

PROCEDURE

1. Extract 0.5g of plant material by homogenizing in 10mL of 3% aqueous sulphosalicylic acid.
2. Filter the homogenate through Whatman No. 2 filter paper.
3. Take 2mL of filtrate in a test tube and add 2mL of glacial acetic acid and 2mL acid ninhydrin.
4. Heat it in the boiling water bath for 1h.
5. Terminate the reaction by placing the tube in ice bath.
6. Add 4mL toluene to the reaction mixture and stir well for 20-30sec.
7. Separate the toluene layer and warm to room temperature.
8. Measure the red color intensity at 520nm.
9. Run a series of standard with pure proline in a similar way and prepare a standard curve.
10. Find out the amount of proline in the test sample from the standard curve.

CALCULATION

Express the proline content on fresh-weight-basis as follows:

$$\text{Proline in n moles per g tissue} = \frac{\text{mg proline/mL} \times \text{mL toluene}}{115.5} \times \frac{5}{\text{g sample}}$$

where 115.5 is the molecular weight of proline.

REFERENCES

Aron D, 1949. Copper Enzymes Isolated Chloroplasts, Polyphenoloxidase in Beta Vulgaris. Plant Physiology. 24: 1-15.

Bates, L.S., Waldren, R.P. & Teare, I.D. Rapid Determination of Free Proline for Water-stress Studies. Plant Soil 39, 205-207 (1973). https://doi.org/10.1007/BF00018060.

Walkley, A. and I.A. Black. 1934. An Examination of Degtjareff Method for Determining Soil Organic Matter and a Proposed Modification of the Chromic Acid Titration Method. Soil Sci. 37: 2 9-37.

Water Analysis

WATER SAMPLING

SITE SELECTION CRITERIA

Ground Water

- Samples for groundwater quality monitoring would be collected from one of the following three types of wells:
  - *Open dug wells* in use for domestic or irrigation water supply
  - *Tube wells* fitted with a hand pump or a power-driven pump for domestic water supply or irrigation
  - *Piezometers*, purpose-built for recording of water level.
- Open dug wells, which are not in use or have been abandoned, will not be considered as water quality monitoring station. However, such wells could be considered for water level monitoring.

Surface Water Rivers/Canals

- The site for which discharge data is available which will provide important information for data analysis and interpretation.

- The site should in general be easily accessible and well maintained.
- Any important changes at or near the site should be noted by the sampling team for use in data interpretation.
- Sampling stations should be located upstream and downstream of significant pollution outfalls.
- Additional downstream stations are necessary to assess the extent of the influence of an outfall, and locate the point of recovery.
- The site can be precisely described (as it is likely that more than one person will need to do the sampling).
- The water body is well mixed both horizontally and vertically at the sampling point.
- The water body at the sampling point is representative of that particular reach or area of water.
- The site is within easy reach of a road (if the sampling team is using a vehicle to get to the site).
- The sampling team normally has to carry an appreciable burden of sampling gear and water samples, and the distance they can walk is limited. Easily accessible sites should be selected. The site should also be accessible under all conditions of weather and river flow. Accessibility is therefore an important consideration.
- Sampling can be carried out away from the bank (on a river, mid-stream/major part of water flow area or near to it is usually preferred.
- The site is inherently safe for sampling.
- Water intake point for community water supply in city/town.
- Presence of large/medium or clusture of small water polluting industries.
- Places of religious bathing (organised).
- Source of river to get indication of its pristine quality.
- Filling up long unrepresented gaps between existing monitoring stations:
  - Large section of irrigated area upstream

- Flow rate/discharge being critical in lean period.
- Downstream of big cities.
- Confluence of tributaries and main river:
  - Inter State boundaries.

Lakes/Reservoirs

- On a lake it is best to sample away from the bank as near-shore points are rarely representative of the bulk of water), middle of the lake or where maximum depth is recorded is preferred site for sampling:
  - Water abstraction point
- Organized bathing.
- In the vicinity of significant out fall(s).
- Recreational spots.
- From the outgoing canal, power channel or water intake structure, in case water is pumped.
- When there is no discharge in the canal, sample will be collected from the upstream side of the regulator structure, directly from the reservoir.
- Depends on the size, shape, depth, bathymetry, wastewater outfall(s), mixing area, mixing gradient, homogeneity etc.

Procedure for Sampling General

- At least one day before sampling, make sure that all the arrangements are made as per the check list.
- Make sure that you know how to reach sampling site(s). Take help of location map for the site which shows the sample collection point with respect to prominent landmarks in the area. In case there is any deviation in the collection point, record it on the sample identification form giving reason.
- Rinse the sample container three times with the sample before it is filled.
- Leave a small air space in the bottle to allow mixing of sample at the time of analysis.

- Label the sample container properly, preferably by attaching an appropriately inscribed tag or label. The sample code and the sampling date should be clearly marked on the sample container or the tag.
- Complete the sample identification forms for each sample, ground and surface water, respectively.
- The sample identification form should be filled for each sampling occasion at a monitoring station. Note that if more than one bottle is filled at a site, this is to be registered on the same form.
- Sample identification forms should all be kept in a master file at the level II or II + laboratory where the sample is analyzed.

Groundwater

- Use a weighted sample bottle to collect sample from an open well about 30 cm below the surface of the water. Do not use a plastic bucket, which is likely to skim the surface layer only.
- Samples from the production tube wells will be collected after running the well for about 5 minutes.
- Non-production piezometers should be purged using a submersible pump. The purged water volume should equal 4 to 5 times the standing water volume, before sample is collected.
- For bacteriological samples, when collected from tube wells/hand pump, the spout/outlet of the pump should be sterilized under flame by spirit lamp before collection of sample in container.

Surface Water

- Samples should be collected from well-mixed section of the river (main stream) 30 cm below the water surface using a weighted bottle or DO sampler.
- Samples from reservoir sites will be collected from the outgoing canal, power channel or water intake structure, in case water is pumped. When there is no discharge in

the canal, sample will be collected from the upstream side of the regulator structure, directly from the reservoir.

- DO is determined in a sample collected in a DO bottle using a DO sampler. The DO in the sample must be fixed immediately after collection, using chemical reagents. DO concentration can then be determined either in the field or later, in a level I or level II laboratory.

Sample Containers, Preservation and Transport

- Use the following type of containers and preservation:

Analysis	Container	Preservation
General	Glass, PE	None
COD, NH_3, NO_2^-, NO_3^-	Glass, PE	H_2SO_4, pH<2
P	Glass	None
DO	BOD bottle	DO fixing chemicals
BOD	Glass, PE	4 °C, dark
Coliform	Glass, PE, Sterilized	4 °C, dark
Heavy metals	Glass, PE	HNO_3, pH<2
Pesticides	Glass, Teflon	4 °C, dark

- Samples should be transported to concerned laboratory as soon as possible, preferably within 48 hours.
- Analysis for coli forms should be started within 24 h of collection of sample. If time is exceeded, it should be recorded with the result.
- Samples containing microgram/L metal level should be stored at 4°C or preserved with nitric acid immediately. If the concentration is of mg/L level, it can be stored for upto 6 months, except mercury, for which the limit is 5 weeks.
- Discard samples only after primary validation of data.

WATER SAMPLING

The objective of water sampling is to collect water, small enough in volume, to be transported conveniently to the laboratory, while, still accurately representing the water source being sampled.

GENERAL PRECAUTIONS

Obtains a sample that meets requirement of the sampling program and handle it in such a way that it does not deteriorate or become contaminated before it reaches the laboratory, Rinse the sampling bottle with the source of water before sampling. Add the preservatives to the sample as per requirement.

Type of Sample

(a) Grab sample: In this case the sample is collected only once

Mixed sample

Fixed quantity of the sample is collected at fixed intervals for a specific period of time irrespective of the water flow.

(b) Composite sampling

Samples are collected in fixed intervals for a specified period of time in relation to the quantity of water discharged. Volume of the sample collected at each time will be proportional to the volume discharged at the specific time of collection.

EXPRESSION OF RESULTS

International System of Units (SI Units) is being followed in the expression of results:

- Anions and Cations are expressed in mg/L
- If desired the results can also be expressed as microgram/L

CALIBRATION OF GLASSWARE

All the glassware to be used in analytical work shall be calibrated as per the standard protocols.

Presently all glassware are calibrated from INDIANA, MOHALI which is NABL accredited.

Records are available along with test certificates in the Lab.

Apart from this, Class-A glassware is used. Their internal calibration is also done. Class B glass wares are also calibrated internally.

1. **TDS, Conductivity Ratio**

$$\text{This accepted criteria is} = \frac{\text{Calculated TDS}}{\text{Conductivity}} = 0.55 \text{ to } 0.9$$

2. **Cation: – Anion Balance**

The percentage difference is defined as $\frac{\sum \text{Cations} - \sum \text{Anions}}{\sum \text{Cations} + \sum \text{Anions}}$ 100-

The criteria for acceptance are

Anionic Sum (m.eq/1)	Acceptable % difference
0.0-3.0	± 0.2 meq./1
3.0-10.0	± 2%
10.0-800.0	± 2n-5%

COLOUR

1. **Purpose**

   To estimate colour of water samples

2. **Scope**

   This Standard prescribes for measurement of colour in the water sample.

3. **Responsibility:** Analyst/Sr. Analyst.

4. **Apparatus:** Nessler Cylinder - 50 ml Capacity

5. **Procedure**

Reference standard of 500 Hazen units on platinum cobalt scale is prepared by dissolving 1.246 gm K_2PtCl_6 and 1.00 gm of $CoCl_2.6H_2O$ in distilled water containing 100 ml of HCL and make up to 1000 ml.

Measurement is made by visually comparing the sample with different standards by diluting the stock solution.

6. **Calculation-Calculate the colour units as follows:**

$$\text{Colour Unit} = \frac{50A}{V}$$

Report the Results in whole numbers as follows:

Colour Units	Record to Nearest
1 to 50	1
51 to 100	5
101 to 250	10
251 to 500	20

TURBIDITY

1. **Purpose**

   To estimate turbidity of water samples

2. **Scope**

   This Standard method prescribes for measurement of turbidity in the water sample.

3. **Chemical Required:**

(a) **Hexamethylene tetramine solution:** Dissolve 10.0 gm of Hexamethylene tetramine in 100ml demineralised water.

(b) **Hydrazine sulphate solution:** Dissolve 1.000 gm Hydrazine Sulphate in 100ml demineralised water.

(c) **Turbidity standard suspension I (Formazine):** in a 100 ml volumetric flask mix 5.0 ml.

(d) Hydrazine sulphate sol. With 5.0ml hexamethylene tetramine solution. After 24-hour standing at 25±3°c, dilute to 100ml with D.M. water and mix well.

(e) **Turbidity standard suspension II:** Dilute 10ml turbidity std. suspension 1 to 100ml with demineralised water. The turbidity of this suspension is defined as 40 NTU.

4. **Procedure**

   The method is based on comparison of the sample with the standard turbidity solutions using a turbidity meter.

The intensity of the scattered light is measured. Higher the intensity, higher will be the turbidity. The results are report in NTU (Nephelometric Turbidity Unit).

5. **Calculation**

$$\frac{A \times (B+C)}{C}$$

TEMPERATURE

1. **Purpose**

To estimate temperature of water samples

2. **Scope**

This Standard method prescribes for measurement of temperature in the water sample.

3. **Procedure:**

(a) Normally temperature measurement may be made with any good mercury filled thermometer. The scale of the thermometer should have a least count of 0.1C.

(b) Make measurement with the thermometer immersed directly in the water body, after a period sufficient to permit contract readings.

(c) Thermometer has been calibrated using standard thermometer periodically and correction factor has to be applied.

pH Value

1. **Purpose**

To estimate pH value of water samples

2. **Scope**

This Standard method prescribes for measurement of pH value in the water sample.

3. **Instrument Required**

- pH meter
- Beaker

4. Chemical Required

(a) DM water

(b) pH - 7.0 buffer solution

(c) pH - 4.0 buffer solution

(d) pH - 9.0 buffer solution

5. Procedure

(a) Electrometric and colorimetric methods are used to measure pH of water sample. Both methods are applicable to all types of water samples.

Electrometric Method

(b) An indicator electrode (pH Electrode) in conjunction with a reference electrode measures pH value. The actual measurement is the electromotive force which is then converted to pH by the instrument.

Calibration

(a) The electrode is to be calibrated every time before the measurement are being made using standard buffer solutions. A series of buffer solutions are used for determination of pH.

6. Reference

Standard Method for the Examination of Water and Wastewater,

IS 3025 (Part-11), 1983 RA1983

Ed. Ed.23rd. 2017; 4500H^+ B.

TOTAL SOLIDS

1. Purpose

To estimate total solids of water samples

2. Scope

This Standard method prescribes for measurement of total solids in the water sample.

3. Procedure

Gravimetric methods are described for the determination of solids. The methods are applicable to all sorts of solids.

TOTAL SOLIDS

Well-shaken known quantity of the sample is dried in a weighed dish in an oven at 98°C. For the constant mass dry the dish at 103-105°C or 179-181°C in an oven. The total residue is calculated from the increased mass.

Total solids is calculated as

Total Solids (mg/1) = 1000 m/v, where M is the mass of the residue and V is the volume of the sample taken.

TOTAL DISSOLVED SOLIDS

The sample is filtered with pore size 2-2.5 μm equivalent to whatman filter No. 542 and the filtrate is dried as in the case of (a). Total Dissolved Solids is as calculated as Total Solids is calculated.

TOTAL SUSPENDED SOLIDS

The filter obtained from the above case is dried to a constant weight in an oven at 103-105°C for one hour. The suspended solids are calculated from the increase in the weight of the filter.

VOLATILE AND FIXED SOLIDS (TOTAL, DISSOLVED AND SUSPENDED)

Total Fixed Solids: The residue obtained in method a) is ignited in muffle furnace at 550°C for one hour. Fixed and volatile solids are calculated from loss in mass on ignition.

(a) **Filterable Fixed solids:** The method is same as above in which the residue to be ignited is from method b)

(b) **Suspended Fixed Solids:** The method is same as above in which the suspended solids are ignited. The correction due destroying of filter paper is also taken into account white calculating the concentration.

CALCULATION FOR FIXED AND VOLATILE SOLIDS

Volatile Solids (mg/1) = (A-B)*1000/V

Fixed Solids (mg/1) = (B-C)*1000/V

Where,

A= Mass in mg of residue and dish/ filter before ignition

B= Mass in mg of residue and dish/ filter after ignition V= Volume of sample

CONDUCTIVITY

1. Purpose

To estimate conductivity of water samples

2. Scope

This Standard prescribes for measurement of conductivity in the water sample.

3. Chemical Required

Standard potassium chloride solution (0.01N): Dissolve 0.7456g KCl dried at 180°C for 1 hour in demineralised water and dilute to 1000ml. The specific conductance of this solution at 25°C is 1408µS/cm.

4. Procedure:

Conductivity is a measure of the ability of an aqueous solution to carry electric current. This ability depends on the presence of ions, total concentrations, mobility and temperature of measurement. It is reciprocal to resistivity.

The conductivity meter is calibrated with standard 0.01N KCL solutions before the measurement is being taken. The cell constant is calculated or adjusted with this standard value. Conductivity of the sample is observed by using calibrated conductivity meter.

Temperature correction is also needed to be applied when measurement of conductivity is being carried out at other temperatures, to arrive at reference temperature.

ACIDITY

1. Purpose

To estimate acidity of water samples

2. Scope

This Standard prescribes for measurement of acidity in the water sample.

3. Chemical Required:

(a) Distilled water

(b) Sodium Hydroxide Solution-0.02N

(c) Phenolphthalein indictor

(d) Methyl Orange Indicator.

4. Procedure

Mineral Acidity (Methyl Orange Acidity)

A suitable volume of the sample is titrated with standard NaOH using methyl orange as indictor. The end point is from orange to yellow color.

Total Acidity (Phenolphthalein Acidity)

In this case the sample is titrated with NaOH using Phenolphthalein indictor. The end point is from colorless to faint pink color.

Calculation

$$\text{Acidity as } CaCO_3 \text{ (mg/1)} = \frac{\text{Vol. of NaOH*Normality of NaOH*50*1000}}{\text{Vol. of Sample taken for titration}}$$

Report result as Acidity to pH (as $CaCO_{3)}$, mg/I

If the sample does not contain silicates, phosphates and borates in significant quantities, the following table be used calculate bicarbonates, carbonates and hydroxyl alkalinities.

ALKALINITY

1. Purpose

To estimate alkalinity of water samples

2. Scope

This Standard prescribes for measurement of alkalinity in the water sample.

3. Chemical Required:

(a) Distilled water

(b) Sulphuric acid solution- 0.02N

(c) Phenolphthalein indicator

(d) Mixed indicator solution- Dissolve 0.02g methyl red and 0.1g bromocresol green in 100ml, 95% ethyl or isopropyl alcohol.

4. Procedure:

Indicator Method:

Pipette 20 ml or a suitable aliquot of sample into 100 ml beaker. If the pH of the sample is over 8.3, then add 2 to 3 drops of phenolphthalein indicator and titrate with standard sulphuric acid till pink color observed by indicator just disappears. Record the volume of std sulphuric acid solution used. Add 2 to 3 drops of mixed indicator to the above solution. Titrate with the std acid to light pink color. Record the volume of std acid used after phenolphthalein alkalinity.

Potentiometric Method: pipette 20ml or a suitable aliquot of sample into 100ml beaker and titrate with std sulphuric acid to pH 8.3 and then to pH 4.5 using pH meter.

Calculation

Phenolphthalein alkalinity (as $CaCO_3$)= AN*50000/V

Total alkalinity (as$CaCO_3$)= (A+B)*N*50000/V

Where,

A = ml of std H_2SO_4 used to titrate to pH 8.3

B = ml of std H_2SO_4 used to titrate from ph 8.3 to pH 4.5

N = normality of acid used

V = volume in ml of sample taken for test

CHLORIDE

1. Purpose

To estimate chloride in water samples

2. Scope

This Standard prescribes for measurement of chloride in the water sample.

3. Chemical Required:

(a) K_2CrO_4 indicator solution -5% w/v (dissolve 50 gm K_2CrO_4 in little distilled water and add $AgNO_3$ solution until a definite red precipitate is found)

(b) Standard. silver nitrate Solution (0.0141 M or N)

(c) Standard sodium chloride (0.0141 M or N)

(d) Aluminum Hydroxide Suspension

(e) Phenolphthalein indicator

(f) Sodium Hydroxide-1N

(g) Sulphuric acid-1N

(h) Hydrogen peroxide -30%

4. Procedure

To a known volume of sample in the pH range 7 to 10, add K_2CrO_4 indicator and titrated with Std. $AgNO_3$ to a reddish yellow end point.

If the sample is colored, add 3 ml aluminum hydroxide suspension, allow settling and filtering it. If sulfide, sulfite or thiosulphate is present, add 1 ml of H_2O_2 and stir well.

Calculation

$$Cl^-, mg/l = \frac{\text{Vol. of } AgNO_3 * \text{Normality of } AgNO_3 * 35.5 * 1000}{\text{Vol. of sample taken}}$$

FLOURIDE

1. **Purpose**

   To estimate fluoride in water samples

2. **Scope**

   This Standard prescribes for measurement of fluoride in the water sample.

3. **Reagents:**

(a) Standard Fluoride Solution-221.0 mg NaF in 1 liter of distilled water. 1ml= 100 μg F.

(b) SPANDS Reagent-960 mg SPADNS in 500 ml distilled water.

(c) Zirocolyl Acid Reagent-133 mg zirconyl chloride in 25 ml distilled water. Add 350 ml conc. HCL and dilute to 500ml.

(d) Mix Solutions 2 & 3.

4. **Procedure**

   Prepare Fluoride standards up to 1.4 mg/l.

   Add 10 ml of the reagent to standards blank and sample.

   Calculate the concentration from the graph.

   If sample contain residual chlorine, remove it by adding Na_2AsO_2.

TOTAL HARDNESS

1. **Purpose**

   To estimate total hardness in water samples

2. **Scope**

   This Standard prescribes for measurement of total hardness in the water sample.

3. **Chemical Required**

(a) Buffer Solution-16.9g NH4Cl and 143 ml conc. NH4OH, 1.179g disodium salt of EDTA and 780 g $MgSO_4.7H_2O$ in 250 ml distilled water.

(b) Erichrome Black T indicator –Mix 0.5g EBT dye and 100 g sodium chloride.

(c) EDTA Solution -0.01M (3.823g EDTA in 1000ml of demineralised water)

5. **Procedure:**

A known quantity of the sample is buffered with 1 ml buffer and titrated with EDTA using the EBT indicator. The end point is from wine red to blue.

Calculation

Vol. of EDTA, ml*Morality of EDTA *100*1000

Total Hardness as CaCO3, mg/1 = Vol. of the sample taken, ml

CALCIUM as Ca

1. **Purpose**

To estimate calcium hardness in water samples

2. **Scope**

This Standard prescribes for measurement of calcium hardness in the water sample.

1. **Chemical Required:**

(a) NaOH - 1N

(b) Murexide indicator-Prepare by mixing 200mg murexide with 100 g NaCl

(c) EDTA Solution -0.01 M

2. **Procedure**

A known quantity of the sample is buffered with 2 ml NaOH and titrated with EDTA using the indicator end the end point is from pink red to purple.

Calculation

$$\text{Calcium as Ca, mg/1} = \frac{\text{Vol. of EDTA} \times \text{Molarity of EDTA} \times 40.08 \times 1000}{\text{Vol. of the sample taken} \times 100}$$

AMMONIA-NITROGEN (NH_3-N)

1. Purpose

To estimate ammonical nitrogen in water samples

2. Scope

This Standard prescribes for measurement of ammonical nitrogen in the water sample.

3. Chemical Required:

(a) Phenol Solution: Mix 11.1 ml liquefied phenol (**89%) with 95% v/v ethyl alcohol to a final volume of 100 ml.

(b) Sodium nitroprusside, 0.5% w/v: Dissolve 0.5 gm sodium nitroprusside in 100 ml deionized water.

(c) Alkaline Citrate: Dissolve 200 gm trisodium citrate and 10 gm sodium hydroxide in deionized water. Dilute to 1000 ml.

(d) Sodium hypochlorite.

(e) Oxidizing solution: Mix 100 ml alkaline citrate solution with 25 ml sodium hypochlorite. Prepare fresh.

(f) Stock Ammonia -3.819 g NH_4Cl in 1000ml. 1 ml= 1mg NH3 –N.

4. Procedure

Take 25 ml of sample in a 50 ml Erlenmeyer flask; add with thoroughly mixing with each addition, 1ml phenol solution, 1 ml sodium nitroprusside solution, and 2.5 ml oxidizing solution. Cover samples with plastic wrap or paraffin wrapper film. Let colour develop at room temperature (22 to 27°C) in subdued light for at least 1 hr. colour is stable for 24 hr. Measure absorbance at 640 nm.

Calculations

Prepare a standard curve by plotting absorbance readings of standards against ammonia concentration of standard. Compute sample concentration by comparing sample absorbance with the standard curve.

NITRATE

1. Purpose

To estimate nitrate in water samples

2. Scope

This Standard prescribes for measurement of nitrate in the water sample.

3. Reagents:

1. Nitrate-free water
2. Stock nitrate solution
3. Standard nitrate solution
4. Sulphite urea reagent
5. Antimony reagent
6. Chromo tropic acid reagent
7. Sulphuric acid

4. Procedure

Pipette 2′0 ml portions of the standard nitrate solutions, samples and a water blank into dry 10 ml volumetric flasks. To each flask, add 1 drop of sulphite-urea reagent. Place flasks in tray of cold water (10 to 20°C) and add 2 ml of antimony reagent. Swirl flasks during addition of each reagent. After about 4 minutes in the bath, add 1 ml of chromo tropic acid reagent. Swirl and let stand in cooling bath for 3 minutes. Add concentrated sulphuric acid to bring volume near the 10 ml mark. Stopper the flasks and mix by inverting each flask four times. Let it stand for 45 minutes at room temperature and adjust volume to 10 ml with concentrated sulphuric acid. Perform final mixing very carefully and gently to avoid introducing gas bubbles. Read absorbance at410 nm between 15 minutes.

$$\text{Nitrate nitrogen (as NOs), mg/l} = \frac{\text{Abs} \times \text{F} \times 1000}{\text{Sample Volume}}$$

NITRITE

1. **Purpose**

   To estimate nitrite in water samples

2. **Scope**

   This Standard prescribes for measurement of nitrite in the water sample.

3. **Chemical Required**

   Sulfanilamide reagent-Dissolve 5.0 g in a mixture of 50 ml conc. HCl and 300 ml distilled water, dilute to 500ml

   NEDA –Dissolve 500mg of NEDA in 500ml of water.

   Hydrochloric Acid 1:3

   Stock Nitrite-1.232 g $NaNO_2$ in 1000ml. Preserve with 1ml of chloroform. 1 ml=250µg of N

4. **Procedure**

   Filter the sample if turbid, adjust the pH to 7.0 and add 1 ml of sulfanilic acid reagent. After 2 minutes add 1 ml NEDA, mix and allow to stand for 10 minutes. Measure the absorbance at 453nm.

   Run the standards and plot a graph. Concentration is calculated from the graph.

SILICA

1. **Purpose**

   To estimate silica in water samples

2. **Scope**

   This Standard prescribes for measurement of silica in the water sample.

Molybdosilicate Method

3. **Chemical Required**

   Sodium Bicarbonate

   Sulphuric Acid -1N

   Hydrochloric acid: 1.1

Ammonium Molybdate Reagent- 100g in 100 ml water (with stirring and gentle warming). Adjust to pH to 7-8 with silica free ammonia or NaOH and store in polyethylene bottle to stabilize.

Oxalic Acid -7.5% w/v in water

Stock Silica Solution

5. Procedure

To 50 ml of blank, series of standards and sample, add 1 ml 1:1 HCl and 2 ml ammonium Molybdate reagent. Mix and after 10 minutes, add 2 ml of oxalic acid solution. Measure the absorbance at 410 nm.

Unreactive Silica

Subtraction of reactive silica from total silica gives Unreactive silica.

For estimating total silica, add 200 mg $NaHCO_3$ to 100 ml of the sample and digest for one hour at 100 °C cool and add 2.4 ml of 1N Sulphuric acid with stirring.

Proceed for estimation of silica as above and calculate the Unreactive silica.

LOW SILICA

Heteropoly Blue Method is used to measure low silica.

Reducing Reagent –Dissolve 500 mg 1-amino-2- naphthol-4- sulphonic acid and one g sodium sulphite in 50 ml distilled silica free water. Add this to a solution of 30 g $NaHSO_3$ in 50 ml water. Filter and keep in a plastic bottle.

6. Procedure

Method to be followed is same as in the previous case. In addition 2 ml reducing reagent is also added. The blue color developed is measured purpose.

To estimate phosphorous in water samples

1. Scope

This Standard prescribes for measurement of phosphorous in the water sample.

2. Chemical Required (Stannous Chloride Method):

1. Strong acid solution- 300ml H_2SO_4 in 600ml water. Add 4 ml HNO_3 and dilute to 1000ml.
2. Ammonium molybdate Reagent -25g ammonium molybdate in 175 distilled water. Add 280ml of conc. sulphuric acid to 400ml of distilled water in a separate beaker, cool and add the molybdate solution to this acid solution and dilute to 1000ml.
3. Stannous Chloride Solution –Dissolve 2.5 g $SnCl_2$ in 100ml glycerol. Heat to dissolve in water bath.
4. Standard Phosphate Solution: dissolve 219.5 mg of anhydrous potassium dihydrogen phosphate in distilled water and dilute to1000ml. 1ml=50μg orthophosphate phosphorus.

3. Procedure

Colored sample to be decolorized with activated carbon.

To 100ml of series of standards, blank and sample, add 4 ml ammonium Molybdate and 0.5 ml stannous chloride. Measure the color at 690 nm.

The concentration is calculated from the graph.

DISSOLVED OXYGEN

1. Purpose

To estimate dissolved oxygen in water samples.

2. Scope

This Standard prescribes for measurement of dissolved oxygen in the water sample.

3. Chemical Required

1. Manganous sulphate Solution -91 g $MnSo_4.H_2O$ in 250 ml water.
2. Alkaline Iodide Azide Reagent –Dissolve 700g KOH (or 500 g NaOH) and 150 g KI or (135g sodium iodide) in freshly boiled and cooled water and dilute to 1 litre. 10g sodium azide in 40 ml water. Mix them together.

3. Conc. H_2SO_4
4. Hypo –N/80
5. Starch Indicator

4. Procedure

Collect the sample in the 300ml DO bottle without any air bubble. Add 2 ml $MnSO_4$ Solution followed by 2ml alkaline iodide azide solution. Shake well by inverting the bottle. Add 2 ml H_2SO_4 and shake well. Titrated with hypo using starch as indicator.

Calculation

$$\text{DO, mg/I} = \frac{\text{Vol. of hypo*normality of hypo*8*1000}}{}$$

SULPHATE

1. Purpose

To estimate sulphate in water samples

2. Scope

This Standard prescribes for measurement of sulphate in the water sample.

Turbidity Method

Sulphate is precipitated in HCL medium with barium chloride as to form barium sulphate crystals of uniform size. Absorption of the suspension is measured at 420 nm.

3. Chemical Required

Conditioning Reagent (1) –Add 0.3 g gelatin in 100 ml water and warm it on hot plate till it is dissolved, keep for 12 hours, add 3.0 g BaCl2 and dissolve by mixing. The turbid solution is kept for 2 hrs. and mixed before use.

1. Condititioning Reagent (II) -50 ml glycerol, 30 ml conc. HCl, 300 ml distilled water, add 100 ml 95% ethanol or isopropyl alcohol and 75 g NaCl.
2. Stock Sulphate solution (100mg/l): Dissolve 0.1479g of anhydrous sodium sulphate in distilled water and dilute to 1 litre.

4. Procedure

Take 20ml of the blank, series of standards, sample or suitable amount diluted to 20ml. Add 1ml 1+9 and 1 ml conditioning reagent and mix. Take the reading after 30 minutes, if conditioning reagent -1 is used or after ten minutes when conditioning reagent – II is used. Take the measurement at 420 nm. Concentration is calculated from the calibration graph.

RESIDUAL CHLORINE

1. Purpose

To estimate residual chlorine in water samples

2. Scope

This Standard prescribes for measurement of residual chlorine in the water sample.

0-Tolidine Method

1. Colour Comparison Method

Colour developed by 0- tolidine is visually compared with standard colour solutions.

3. Chemical Required

1. Dil. HCL-1.9
2. O-Tolidine Solution 1.35 g g 0-tolidine dihydrochloride in 1000 ml dil. HCl.
3. $CuSO_4$ Solution -1.5 g in 1000 ml water containing 1 ml H2SO4.
4. K_2Cr2O_7 Solution -0.25 g in 1000 ml water containing 1 ml H2SO4
5. Sodium Arsenite Solution -0.5 g in 1000 ml water.

Standard Color Solution – to be prepared as given below. Final Volume -100 ml.

4. Procedure

Take three cylinders A, B, C. In A, add 1 ml tolidine reagent, 100 ml sample, mixadd 2 ml arsenite reagent. Compare the colour after 2 minutes (FR). In B, add 2 ml arsenite solution, 100 ml sample, mix and add 1 ml tolidine reagent. Mix and campare the colour after 2 minutes (B1). Again take the reading 15 minutes (B2). In C, add 1 ml tolidine reagent and 100 ml water and take reading after 15 minutes (TR)

Calculation

- Free Residual Chlorine, mg/1= FR-B1
- Total Residual Chlorine, mg/1 = TR-B2

Combined Residual Chlorine, mg/I = (TR-B2)-(FR-B1).

a) Stabilized Neutral O-Tolidine Method.

Reagents

Distilled Water

Neutral o-tolidine reagent-5 ml HCl to 500 ml water. Add 10 ml of this solution, 20 mg HgC12, 30 mg EDTA and 1.5 g o-tolidine reagent and dilute to 1000 ml. Store in a brown bottle.

Buffer Stabilizer reagent- 34.4 g K_2HPO_4, 12.6 KH_2PO_4 and 8 g solid di (2-ethl hexyl) sulpho succinate in 500 ml water and add 200 ml diethylene glycol mono butyl ether. Dilute to 1000 ml.

1. KI Solution -0.4%
2. Sulphuric acid -0.4 ml to 100 ml water.
3. Sodium Carbonate-5 g in 100 ml
4. Sodium Arsenite-5.0 g in 1000ml
5. Standard Chlorine Solution

5. Procedure

5 ml tolidine reagent and 5 ml stabilizer reagent in 100 ml sample\. Measure the value

Spectrophotometrically (A) Monochloramine

Add 0.5 ml KI Solution with stirring and measure the value (B) Dichloramine

Add 1 ml sulphuruic acid, after 30 seconds, add 1 ml sodium carbonate solution and measure the colour.

Calculation

Free Residual Chlorine, mg/l = A, including ½ trichloramine, if present

Monochloramine, mg/l = (B-A) as mg/l chlorine Dichloramine, mg/l = 1.06C –B AS ms/l chlorine Total

Chlorine, mg/l = 1.03C as mg/l chlorine.

Iodometric Method

Iodine is liberated by adding KI and is titrated with hypo using starch as indicator.

Reagents

1. Glacial Acetic Acid
2. KI Crystals
3. Standard Hypo Solution
4. Starch Indicator

Procedure

Acidify the sample with acetic acid and add few crystals of KI. Titrated with standard hypo using starch as indicator, until the blue colour is discharged.

Calculation

$$\text{Residual Chlorine, mg/l} = \frac{\text{Vol. of Hypo*Normality of Hypo*35.45*1000}}{\text{Vol. of sample taken}}$$

BORON

1. **Purpose**

   To estimate boron in water samples

2. **Scope**

   This Standard prescribes for measurement of boron in the water sample.

3. **Colorimetric Curcumin Method**

   Principle

   The sample is evaporated to dryness in the presence of NaOH. Curcumin in acetic acid is added to it. On acidification with acetic acid-sulphuric acid, Curcumin reacts with boric acid forming a colored complex. The un-reacted curcumin is removed with acetone and water mixture.

Chemical Required

1. Curcumin reagent -0.125% in glacial acetic acid.
2. Sulphuric acid –acetic acid mixture-1.1
3. Standard Boron Solution.
4. Acetone Water Mixture-1:1
5. NaOH-1.0%

5. Procedure

Sample, Standards and blanks containing 1 ml NaOH is evaporated to dryness. Add 3 ml curcumin reagent, warm to dissolve the residue. Cool and add 1.5 ml reagent no. 2 and keep for 15 minutes. Dilute to 50 ml with reagent No.4 Measure the absorbance at 555 nm.

SODIUM & POTASSIUM

1. Purpose

To estimate sodium & potassium in water samples

2. Scope

This Standard prescribes for measurement of sodium & potassium in the water sample.
Flame Photometry Method

3. Chemical Required

Na CRM
K CRM

4. Procedure

Results will be come directly from the Fame photometer.
IS: 3025 (Part- 45)

BIOCHEMICAL OXYGEN DEMAND

1. Purpose

To estimate biochemical oxygen demand in water samples.

2. Scope

This Standard prescribes for measurement of biochemical oxygen demand in the water sample.

3. Chemical Required

1. Phosphate buffer-8.5 g KH_2PO_4, 21.75 g Na_2HPO_4 and 1.7 g NH_4Cl in 1000 ml.
2. $MgSO_4$ solution. 22.5 g MgSO4.7H_2O in 1000ml.
3. $CaCl_2$ solution: 27.5 g in 1000 ml.
4. $FeCl_3$ solution 0.25 g $FeCl_3.6H_2O$ in 1000 ml
5. Acid and alkali solution 1 N H_2SO_4 & 1 N NaOH.
6. Na_2SO_4 solution -1.575 g in 1000 ml prepare daily.
7. Glucose –Glutamic acid solution -150 mg glucose and 150 g glutamic acid (dried at 103°C for 1 h) in 1000 ml.
8. Ammonium Chloride -1.15 g in 500 ml. Adjust to pH 7.2 and make up to 1000 ml.

4. Procedure

Preparation of dilution water

The water is saturated with oxygen by bubbling. Allow it to stabilize overnight in the incubator. Add 1 ml each of reagents 1 to 4 shakes well. Seed the dilution water if necessary. Periodically check the dilution water.

BOD determination

Make different dilutions in duplicate and fill with dilution water in do bottles. Care must be taken that no air bubble is trapped in the bottle. Determine IDOD in one set of samples. The other set is incubated. After the incubation again find the DO.

Calculations

BOD, mg/l = IDOD-DO after incubation*dilution factor.

Pre treatment of sample

- Adjust the sample pH to normal
- Remove the free chlorine; if present, by calculated addition of Hypo Glucose –glutamic acid check

Glucose –glutamic acid mixture has a specific BOD. The correctness of analysis can be checked with this solution.

If the BOD of dilution water is more than 1.5 mg/l. prepare fresh dilution water. If seeding is done, apply the correction factor.

CHEMICAL OXYGEN DEMAND

1. Purpose

To estimate chemical oxygen demand in water samples.

2. Scope

This Standard prescribes for measurement of chemical oxygen demand in the water sample.

3. Chemical Required

1. Mercuric sulphate Crystals
2. Sulphuric acid-Silver Nitrate Reagent -10.2 g in 1000 ml acid
3. K2Cr2O7-0.25 N: Dissolve 12.259g potassium dichromate previously dried at 105°C for 24h, in distilled water. Add 120mg sulphamic acid to this. Dilute to 1 ltr.
4. FAS-0.1 N: Dissolve 39g FAS in distilled water. Add 20ml sulphuric acid, dilute to 1 liter. Standardize this solution daily against $K_2Cr_2O_7$

   1. Ferroin indicator -695 g ferrous sulphate & 1.485 g 1-10 phenanthroline in 100 ml water.

4. Procedure

To a known quantity of sample, add Sulphuric acid reagent, add 1 g mercuric Sulphate to complex the precipitated chloride. Add a know quantity of dichromate and reflux for 2 hrs.

Run a blank also. When cooled, titrated with FAS using Ferroin indicator. Near the end of the titration color changes from green blue to wine red.

Calculations

$$\text{COD, mg/l} = \frac{\text{(Blank-sample titer value)*normality of FAS*8*1000}}{\text{Vol. of the sample}}$$

Interferences

When chloride is more than 2000mg/l, do not do COD. Nitrate interference can be removed by adding 10 mg sulphamic acid, before adding dichromate.

PHENOLIC COMPOUNDS

1. Purpose

To estimate phenolic compound in water samples

2. Scope

This Standard prescribes for measurement of phenolic compound in the water sample.

3. Chemical Required

1. Bromide-Bromate Solution -2.784 KBro3 and 10 g KBr in 1000 ml water.
2. HCl
3. Ammonia –ammonium Chloride Buffer -16.9 g NH4Cl in 143 ml NH3 dilute to 250 ml.
4. 4-Amino Antipyrene-2%
5. Potassium Ferricyanide 8%
6. Chloroform
7. Sodium Sulphate
8. Phenol Stock: Dissolve 1.0g phenol in freshly boiled and cooled distilled water and dilute to 1000ml.

4. Procedure

To 500ml of a series of standards, blank and the samples in separating funnels, add 3 ml 4-aminoantipyrene solution, 3 ml ferricyanide and shake well. Allow to stand for 2-3 minutes Extract the color with chloroform. Measure the absorbance at 460 nm.

Plot a calibration graph. Calculate the concentration in the sample from the graph.

FREE CARBON DIOXIDE

1. Purpose

To estimate of Free Carbon dioxide samples

2. Scope

This Standard prescribes for measurement of Free Carbon dioxide in the water sample.

3. Chemical Required

1. Distilled water.
2. Sodium Hydroxide solution-0.02 N
3. Phenolphthalein indicator

4. Procedure

A suitable volume of the sample is titrated with NaOH using phenolphthalein indicator to end point from colour less to faint pink colour (pH -8.3)

In case from coloured sample the titration is carried with the use of a pH meter

Calculations

$$\text{Free Carbon dioxide as } CO_2 = \frac{\text{Vol of NaOH*Normality of NaOH*44*1000}}{\text{Vol. of the sample taken}}$$

ARSENIC as As

1. **Purpose** The purpose of this protocol is to provide guidelines for monitoring and calculation of arsenic from stationary sources.
2. **Scope: This** Standard method prescribes for measurement of arsenic from the stationary source.
3. **Range and sensitivity:** This method is applicable in the range from 0.01 to 2·0 mg/l.
4. **Instrument Required**

1. Atomic absorption spectrometer
2. Atomizer
3. Arsenic Hydride

Chemical Required

A. **Sodium borohydride reagent:** Dissolve 8 g sodium borohydride in 200 ml of 0.1 N sodium: hydroxide solution. Prepare fresh daily.

B. **Sodium iodide pre-reductant solution:** Dissolve 50 g of sodium iodide in 500 ml water. Prepare fresh daily.

C. **Sulphuric acid:**18 N

D. **Sulphuric acid:** 2.5 N

E. **Potassium persulphate:** 5 percent solution, Dissolve 25 gm of potassium persulphate in water and dilute to 500 ml. Store in glass and refrigerate, Prepare weekly.

F. **Nitric acid**: Concentrated

G. **Perch/oric acid:** Concentrated.

H. **Hydrochloric acid:** Concentrated.

I. **Argon (or nitrogen):** Commercial grade.

J. **Arsen ic (III)** *solutions*

K. Stock arsenic (III) solution

Procedure

Setting up of apparatus: According to manufacturer's instructions, connect inlet of reaction cell with auxiliary purging gas by flow meter. If a drying cell between there action cell and atomizer is necessary, use only anhydrous calcium chloride but not calcium sulphate. Before using the hydride generation/analysis. system, optimize operating parameters, Aspirate aqueous solutions of arsenic directly into the flame to facilitate atomizer alignment, Align quartz atomizers for maximum absorbance. Establish purging gas flow concentration and rate of addition of sodium borohydride reagent solution volume and rate of the stirring for optimum instrument response. If quartz atomizer is used, optimize cell temperature. The recommended wavelength is 193'7 nm for arsenic.

Calculations

Construct a standard curve by plotting peak heights of standards *versus* concentration of standards. Measure peak heights of samples and read concentrations from the curve. If sample was diluted before digestion, apply an appropriate factor.

CADMIUM as Cd

1. **Purpose:** The purpose of this protocol is to provide guidelines for monitoring and calculation of cadmium from stationary sources.
2. **Scope:** This Standard method prescribes for measurement of cadmium from the stationary source.
3. **Principle**

   This cadmium content of the sample is determined by directly aspirating the sample into the flame of an atomic absorption spectrophotometer. The absorbance is measured at 228.8 nm using a cadmium hollow-cathode lamp.
4. **Range and sensitivity:** This method is applicable in the range from 0·05 to 0.2 mg/l.

5. Instrument Required

1. Atomic absorption spectrophotometer with air-acetylene flame.
2. Cadmium hollow-cathode lamp

6. Chemical Required

Hydroc

Hydrochloric Acid - Concentrated. Nitric Acid - Concentrated Nitric Acid - Diluted (1: 499).

Cadmium Solutions

Stock cadmium solution

7. Procedure

1. To 100 ml portion of the acidified sample add 5 ml of concentrated hydrochloric acid and evaporate to 20 ml. Cool and filter the sample and make up to 100 ml in a standard flask. If only dissolved cadmium is to be flask. If only dissolved cadmium is to be determined, filter

100 ml of the sample and determined, filter 100 ml of the sample and determined, filter 100 ml of the sample and Acidify with 0·1 ml of Conc.HCL acid. Aspirate the sample solution and measure the absorbance at 228.8 nm.

2. Prepare a reagent blank and a series of100 ml standards containing 0.0, 0-.05, 0.1, 0.5, 1 and 2 mg/l of cadmium by diluting a suitable volume of the standard solution with dilute nitric acid and repeat as above. Aspirate the solutions and measure the absorbance.

Calculations

Construct a standard calibration graph by plotting the absorbance versus cadmium concentration (mg/I) of each standard. Read the concentration of the sample from the graph.

Cadmium, mg/l = $V \times 1000$

Where

M = mass of cadmium in mg in the sample, and

V = volume of the sample in ml.

COPPER as Cu

1. **Purpose:** The purpose of this protocol is to provide guidelines for monitoring and calculation of copper from stationary sources.
2. **Scope:** This Standard method prescribes for measurement of copper from the stationary source.
3. **Principle:** The copper content of the sample is determined by atomic absorption spectrophotometry. For dissolved Copper, the filtered sample is directly aspirated Into the atomizer.
4. **Range and sensitivity:** This method is applicable in the range from *0.2* to 5 *mg/l.*
5. **Instrument Required**

1. Atomic Absorption Spectrophotometer with air-acetylene flame.
2. Copper Hollow Cathode Lamp - for use a 324·7 nm.

6. Chemical Required

Hydrchloric Acid - Concentrated Nitric Acid - Concentrated.

Dilute Nitric Acid - 1 : 500.

Dilute Sulphuric Acid - I : 1. Copper (II) S

Solutions

Stock copper (II) solution

Standard copper (11) solution

Procedure

If total recoverable copper is to be determined, add 5 ml of concentrated hydrochloric acid and evaporate the solution to IS to 20 mi. Cool and filter the sample through acid washer filter paper. Make up to 100 ml in a volumetric flask, aspirate the solution and measure the absorbance at 324.7 nm using copper hollow - cathode lamp. Aspirate nitric acid (1: 500) prior to sample aspiration. Prepare a reagent blank and series of standards containing 0, 0.02, 0·1, 0.5, 1,2,5 mg/l of copper by diluting a suitable volume of the standard solution with 100 all of nitric. acid (1: 500) and repeat as above. Aspirate the solutions and measure the absorbance.

Calculations

Construct a standard calibration graph by plotting the absorbance versus copper concentration (mg/l) for each standard. Read the concentration of the sample from the graph:

$$\text{Copper, mg/I} = \frac{M \times 1000}{V}$$

Where

M = mass (in g) of copper in the sample, and $_V$ =

LEAD as Pb

1. **Purpose:** The purpose of this protocol is to provide guidelines for monitoring and calculation of lead from stationary sources.

2. **Scope:** This Standard method prescribes for measurement of lead from the stationary source.
3. **Principle:** The lead content of the sample is determined by direttly aspirating the sample into the flame ofan atomic absorption spectrophotometer.
4. **Range and sensitivity:** This method is applicable in the range from 1·0 to 10.0 mg/l of lead.
5. **Instrument Required:**
1. Atomic absorption spectrophotometer with air-acetylene flame.
2. Hollow-cathode lamps or electrode less discharge lamps for use at 283′3 nm.
6. **Chemical Required**

   Hydrochloric Acid - Concentrated Nitric Acid - Concentrated Nitric Acid - Diluted (1 : 499).

   Lead Solutions

   Stock lead solution

Procedure

To 100 ml portion of the acidified sample add 20 ml of nitric acid, 5.0 ml of concentrated hydrochloric acid and heat it not to boil but to reduce the volume to 20 ml in a well-ventilated hood. Cool and filter the sample and make upto 100 ml in a standard flask. Aspirate the sample solution and measure the absorbance at 283·3 nm. Aspirate nitric acid (1 : 499) prior to sample aspiration.

Prepare a reagent blank and sufficient standards containing 1.0, 2.5, 5.0, 7·5 and 10·0 mg/. of lead by diluting suitable volume of the standard solution with nitric acid (I : 499)and repeat as above. Aspirate the solutions and measure the absorbance.

Calculations

Construct a standard calibration graph by plotting the absorbance versus mg of lead concentration of each standard. Read the concentration of the sample from the graph.

$$\text{Lead, } (mg/l) = \frac{M \times 1000}{V}$$

Where

M = - mass_0 lead present in mg in the sample, and

V = volume of sample

SELENIUM as Se

1. **Purpose:** The purpose of this protocol is to provide guidelines for monitoring and calculation of selenium from stationary sources.
2. **Scope:** This Standard method prescribes for measurement of selenium from the stationary source.
3. **Responsibility:** Analyst/Sr. Analyst.
4. **Principle:** The method is based on the atomic absorption spectrometric measurement of selenium generated by the thermal decomposition of selenium hydride. Under the conditions of this method, only Se (IV) is quantitatively converted to the hydride.
5. **Range and sensitivity:** This method is applicable in the range at a wavelength of 196.0 nm.
6. **Instrument Required**

1. Atomic Absorption Spectrometer.
2. Gas Supply – with argon or nitrogen.
3. Glas sware.

7. **Chemical Required**

Sulphuric Acid—p = 1.84 g/ml.

Hydrochloric Acid--p = 1.16 g/ml.

Hydrogen Peroxide — w (H202) = 30 percent (m/m).

Sodium Hydroxide

Sodium Tetrahydroborate Solution

Selenium, Stock Solution

Selenium, Standard Solution 1 Selenium, Standard Solution 2

7. **Procedure**

Blank Solution

Pipette 2 ml of hydrochloric acid into a graduated flask of nominal capacity 100 ml, and dilute to volume with water. Treat the blank in exactly the same way as the sample.

1. Method of digestion

Add 5 ml of sulphuric acid (see 7.4.1) and 5 ml of hydrogen peroxide to the round-bottomed flask . Add some boiling beads and connect the flask to an apparatus close the cock. Heat the contents of the flask to boiling and collect the condensate in the condensate reservoir. Continue heating until turbid fumes of sulphuric acid appear. Check the appearance of the sample. [Fit is turbid and almost colorless, cool and adds another 5 ml of hydrogen peroxide and continues boiling as described above. After cooling, return the condensate to the round bottomed flask.

Evaluation of Results

Obtain the mass concentration of Se in microgram /l. in the measurement solution on the basis of absorbance and the calibration function.

ZINC as Zn

1. **Purpose:** The purpose of this protocol is to provide guidelines for monitoring and calculation of zinc from stationary sources.
2. **Scope:** This Standard method prescribes for measurement of zinc from the stationary source.
3. **Principle:** The zinc content of the sample is determined by atomic Absorption spectrophotometer For dissolved zinc, the filtered sample is directly aspirated to the atomizer. For total recoverable zinc, an acid digestion procedure is done prior to aspiration of the sample.
4. **Range and sensitivity:** This method is applicable in the range from 0.01 to 2·0 mg/l.
5. **Instrument Required**

1. Atomic Absorption Spectrophotometer, with Air-Acetylene Flame

2. Multi-element hollow-cathode lamps or electrode less discharge lamps for use at 213.8 nm.

6. **Chemical Require**

Hydrochloric Acid - Concentrated. Nitric Acid - Concentrate

Nitric Acid - Diluted (1 : 499)

Zinc (II) Solution

Stock zinc (11) solution

Procedure: Add 0·5 ml of nitric acid to 100 ml of the sample (filtered or unfiltered). If total recoverable zinc is to be determined, add *S* ml of concentrated hydrochloric acid and filter the sample through acid washed filter paper. Make up to 100 ml in a volumetric flask, aspirate the solution and measure the absorbance at 213·8 nm, Aspirate nitric acid (1 : 499) prior to nm, Aspirate nitric acid (1 : 499) prior to sample aspiration.

2 Prepare a reagent blank and sufficient standards containing 0.01, 0.05, 0·1, 0.5, 1·0 and 2·0 mg/l of zinc by diluting suitable volume of the standard solution with nitric acid (1: 499) and repeat as above. Aspirate the solutions and measure the absorbance.

Calculations

1 Construct a standard calibration graph by plotting the absorbance versus standard concentration for each standard. Read the concentration of the samples from the graph.

$$\text{Zinc, } (mg/l)) = \frac{M \times 1000}{V}$$

M = mass of zinc present in mg in sample,

V= volume of sample in ml.

REFERENCES

Standard Method for the Examination of Water and Wastewater IS 3025 (Part-16) 1984, RA 2006 Ed. Ed.23rd. 2017; 4500H^+ B.

Standard Method for the Examination of Water and Wastewater, IS 3025 (Part-14) 1984, RA 2002 Edi. Ed.23rd. 2017; 2510 B.

6

Air Quality Analysis

GUIDELINES FOR SAMPLING AND MEASUREMENT OF NOTIFIED AMBIENT AIR QUALITY PARAMETERS (NAAQS 2009)

Under the provisions of the Air (Prevention & Control of Pollution) Act, 1981, the CPCB has notified fourth version of National Ambient Air Quality Standards (NAAQS) in 2009. This revised national standard aims to provide uniform air quality for all, irrespective of land use pattern, across the country. There are 12 identified health based parameters, which are to measure at the national level and with a view to have data comparison, need for uniform guidelines for monitoring, sampling, analyses, sample flow chart, data sheet based on standard method has been felt.

The methods prescribed in the notification for respective parameters are the combination of physical method, wet-chemical method and continuous on-line method. Therefore, to meet the NAAQS requirement, a combination of both manual and continuous method is invariably required at each monitoring location, besides good laboratory set up and infrastructure.

In addition to the above, an in house exercise for applicability of all prescribed/recommended analytical methods was also felt necessary. After review and demonstration in the Central Laboratory, Delhi, guidelines are being prepared and documented in next page.

1. Volume-I: Guidelines for manual sampling and analyses (along with sample flow chart and data sheets);
2. Volume-II: Guidelines for continuous sampling and real time analyses;
3. Volume-III: Reference methods for manual sampling and analyses (compilation)
4. Volume-IV: Reference methods for continuous sampling and real time analyses (compilation)

NATIONAL AMBIENT AIR QUALITY STANDARDS (2009)

Pollutants	Time Weighted Average	Concentration in Ambient Air		Methods of Measurement
		Industrial, Residential, Rural and other Areas	Ecologically Sensitive Area (Notified by Central Government)	
Sulphur Dioxide (SO_2), μg/m^3	Annual* 24 Hours**	50 80	20 80	- Improved West and Gaeke Method - Ultraviolet Fluorescence
Nitrogen Dioxide (NO_2), μg/m^3	Annual * 24 Hours**	40 80	30 80	- Jacob & Hochheiser modified ($NaOH$-$NaAsO_2$) Method - Gas Phase Chemiluminescence
Particulate Matter (Size less than 10μm) or PM_{10}, μg/m^3	Annual* 24 Hours**	60 100	60 100	- Gravimetric - TEOM - Beta attenuation

(Contd…)

Pollutants	Time Weighted Average	Concentration in Ambient Air		Methods of Measurement
		Industrial, Residential, Rural and other Areas	Ecologically Sensitive Area (Notified by Central Government)	
Particulate Matter (Size less than 2.5µm) or $PM_{2.5}$, µg/m³	Annual * 24 Hours**	40 60	40 60	- Gravimetric - TEOM - Beta attenuation
Ozone (O_3) µg/m³	8 Hours* 1 Hour**	100 180	100 180	- UV Photometric - Chemiluminescence - Chemical Method
Lead (Pb) µg/m³	Annual* 24 Hours**	0.50 1.0	0.50 1.0	- AAS/ICP Method after sampling on EPM 2000 or equivalent filter paper - ED-XRF using Teflon filter
Carbon Monoxide(CO), mg/m³	8 Hours ** 1 Hour **	02 04	02 04	- Non dispersive Infrared (NDIR) Spectroscopy
Ammonia (NH_3), µg/m³	Annual* 24 Hours**	100 400	100 400	- Chemiluminescence - Indophenol blue method
Benzene (C_6H_6), µg/m³	Annual*	05	05	- Gas Chromatography (GC) based continuous analyzer - Adsorption and desorption followed by GC analysis

(Contd...)

Pollutants	Time Weighted Average	Concentration in Ambient Air		Methods of Measurement
		Industrial, Residential, Rural and other Areas	Ecologically Sensitive Area (Notified by Central Government)	
Benzo(a) Pyrene (BaP) Particulate phase only, ng/m^3	Annual*	01	01	- Solvent extraction followed by HPLC/GC analysis
Arsenic (As), ng/m^3	Annual*	06	06	- AAS/ICP Method after sampling on EPM 2000 or equivalent filter paper
Nickel (Ni), ng/m^3	Annual*	20	20	- AAS/ICP Method after sampling on EPM 2000 or equivalent filter paper

*Annual Arithmetic mean of minimum 104 measurements in a year at a particular site taken twice a week 24 hourly at uniform intervals.

**24 hourly or 8 hourly or 1 hourly monitored values, as applicable, shall be complied with 98% of the time in a year. 2% of the time, they may exceed the limits but not on two consecutive days of monitoring.

Note: Whenever and wherever monitoring results on two consecutive days of monitoring exceed the limits specified above for the respective category, it shall be considered adequate reason to institute regular or continuous monitoring and further investigations.

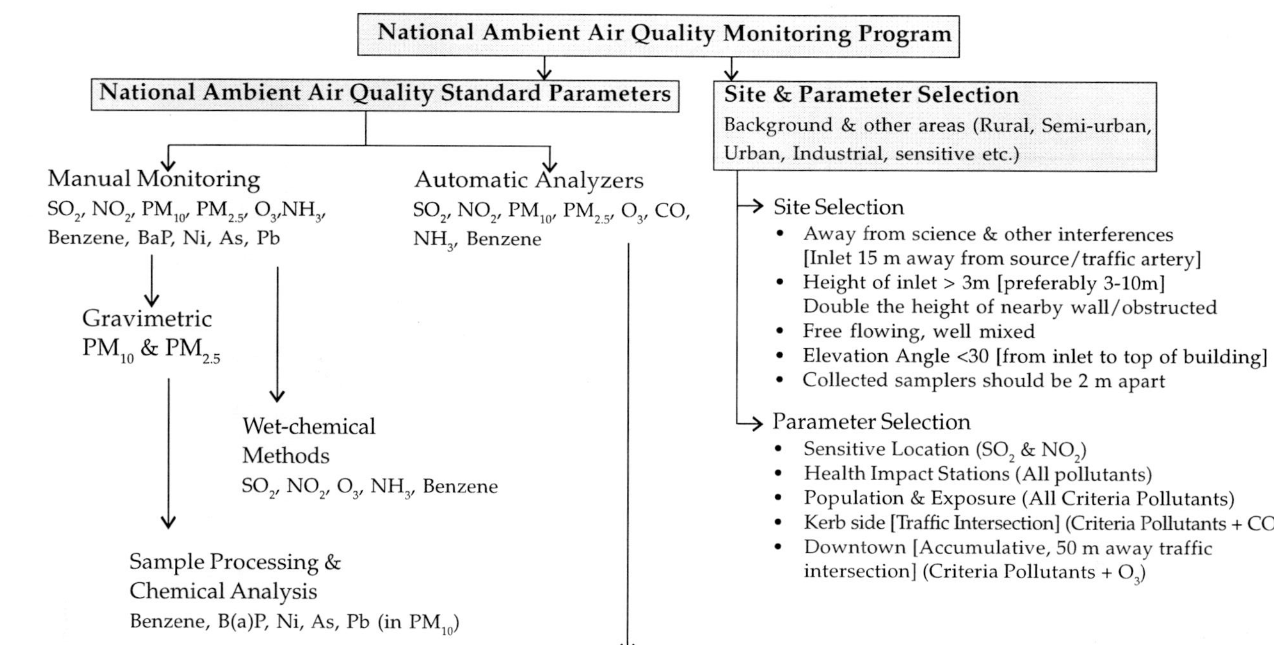
National Ambient Air Quality Monitoring Program
National Ambient Air Quality Standard Parameters
Site & Parameter Selection
Background & other areas (Rural, Semi-urban, Urban, Industrial, sensitive etc.)
Manual Monitoring
SO_2, NO_2, PM_{10}, $PM_{2.5}$, O_3, NH_3, Benzene, BaP, Ni, As, Pb
Automatic Analyzers
SO_2, NO_2, PM_{10}, $PM_{2.5}$, O_3, CO, NH_3, Benzene
Site Selection
• Away from science & other interferences [Inlet 15 m away from source/traffic artery]
• Height of inlet > 3m [preferably 3-10m] Double the height of nearby wall/obstructed
• Free flowing, well mixed
• Elevation Angle <30 [from inlet to top of building]
• Collected samplers should be 2 m apart
Gravimetric
PM_{10} & $PM_{2.5}$
Wet-chemical Methods
SO_2, NO_2, O_3, NH_3, Benzene
Parameter Selection
• Sensitive Location (SO_2 & NO_2)
• Health Impact Stations (All pollutants)
• Population & Exposure (All Criteria Pollutants)
• Kerb side [Traffic Intersection] (Criteria Pollutants + CO)
• Downtown [Accumulative, 50 m away traffic intersection] (Criteria Pollutants + O_3)
Sample Processing & Chemical Analysis
Benzene, B(a)P, Ni, As, Pb (in PM_{10})
Well established monitoring cum-laboratory infrastructure, Trained manpower, Well established guidelines, manual data generation & dissemination etc.
Sophisticated Analyzers, QA/QC, Instant Data Generation, On line data disseminations, Air Quality Index, Early Warning System, Forecasting, Modeling etc.

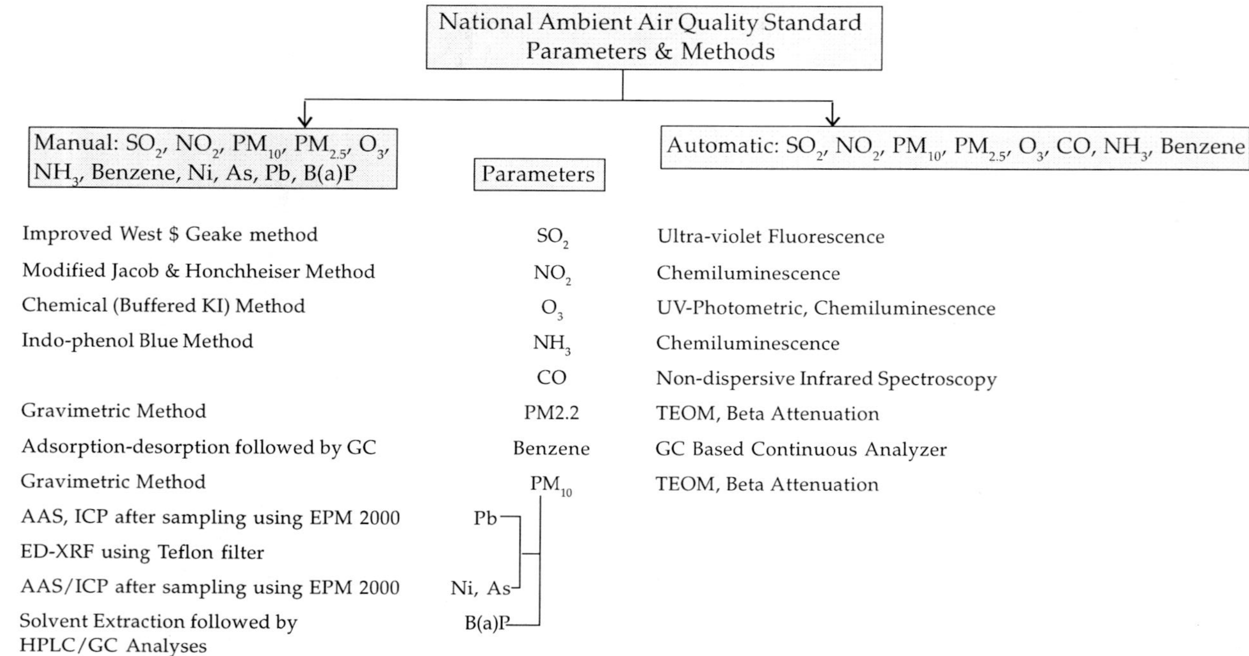
National Ambient Air Quality Monitoring Program
National Ambient Air Quality Standard Parameters & Methods
Manual: SO_2, NO_2, PM_{10}, $PM_{2.5}$, O_3, NH_3, Benzene, Ni, As, Pb, B(a)P
Parameters
Automatic: SO_2, NO_2, PM_{10}, $PM_{2.5}$, O_3, CO, NH_3, Benzene
Improved West $ Geake method
SO_2
Ultra-violet Fluorescence
Modified Jacob & Honchheiser Method
NO_2
Chemiluminescence
Chemical (Buffered KI) Method
O_3
UV-Photometric, Chemiluminescence
Indo-phenol Blue Method
NH_3
Chemiluminescence
CO
Non-dispersive Infrared Spectroscopy
Gravimetric Method
PM2.2
TEOM, Beta Attenuation
Adsorption-desorption followed by GC
Benzene
GC Based Continuous Analyzer
Gravimetric Method
PM_{10}
TEOM, Beta Attenuation
AAS, ICP after sampling using EPM 2000
Pb
ED-XRF using Teflon filter
AAS/ICP after sampling using EPM 2000
Ni, As
Solvent Extraction followed by HPLC/GC Analyses
B(a)P

GUIDELINES FOR SAMPLING AND ANALYSIS OF SULPHUR DIOXIDE IN AMBIENT AIR (IMPROVED WEST AND GAEKE METHOD)

PURPOSE

The purpose of this protocol is to provide guidelines for monitoring and analysis of sulphur dioxide in ambient air.

STANDARD

The national ambient air quality standards for sulphur dioxide is presented in the table

Pollutant	Time Weighted Average	Concentration in Ambient Air	
		Industrial, Residential, Rural and other Areas	Ecologically Sensitive Area (Notified by Centra Government)
Sulphur Dioxide (SO_2), $\mu g/m^3$	Annual* 24 Hours**	50 80	20 80

*Annual Arithmetic mean of minimum 104 measurements in a year, at a particular site, taken twice a week 24 hourly at uniform intervals.

**24 hourly or 8 hourly or 1 hourly monitored values, as applicable, shall be complied with 98% of the time in a year. 2% of the time, they may exceed the limits but not on two consecutive days of monitoring.

PRINCIPLE OF THE METHOD

Modified West & Gaeke Method (IS 5182 Part 2 Method of Measurement of Air Pollution: Sulphur dioxide).

Sulphur dioxide from air is absorbed in a solution of potassium tetrachloromercurate (TCM). A dichlorosulphitomercurate complex, which resists oxidation by the oxygen in the air, is formed. Once formed, this complex is stable to strong oxidants such as ozone and oxides of nitrogen and therefore, the absorber solution may be stored for some time prior to analysis. The complex is made to react with para-rosaniline and formaldehyde to form the intensely coloured pararosaniline methylsulphonic acid. The absorbance of the solution is measured by means of a suitable spectrophotometer.

INSTRUMENT/EQUIPMENT

The following items are necessary to perform the monitoring and analysis of nitrogen dioxide in ambient air:

- Analytical balance
- Vacuum pump: Capable of maintaining an air pressure differential greater than 0.7 atmosphere at the desired flow rate
- Calibrated flow-measuring device to control the airflow from 0.2 to 1 l/min.
- Absorber: all glass midget impinger
- Spectrophotometer: Capable of measuring absorbance at 560 nm equipped with 1 cm path length cells.
- Glass wares: low actinic glassware must be used for analysis

REAGENTS/CHEMICALS

All the chemicals should meet specifications of Analytical Reagent grade.

- Distilled water
- Mercuric chloride
- Potassium chloride/Sodium chloride
- EDTA di sodium salt
- Absorbing Reagent, 0.04 M Potassium Tetrachloro mercurate (TCM) - Dissolve 10.86 g, mercuric chloride, 0.066 g EDTA, and 6.0 g potassium chloride or sodium chloride 4.68 gm in water and bring to the mark in a 1 litre volumetric flask. *Caution : highly poisonous if spilled on skin, flush off with water immediately*. The pH of this reagent should be approximately 4.0 but, it has been shown that there is no appreciable difference in collection efficiency over the range of pH 5 to pH 3. The absorbing reagent is normally stable for six months. If, a precipitate forms, discard the reagent after recovering the mercury.
- Sulphamic Acid (0.6%) - Dissolve 0.6 g sulphamic acid in 100 ml distilled water. Prepare fresh daily.

- Formaldehyde (0.2%) - Dilute 5 ml formaldehyde solution (36-38%) to 1 litre with distilled water. Prepare fresh daily.
- Purified Pararosaniline Stock Solution (0.2% Nominal) Dissolve 0.500 gm of specially purified pararosaniline (PRA) in 100 ml of distilled water and keep for 2 days (48 hours).
- Pararosaniline Working Solution - 10 ml of stock PRA is taken in a 250 ml volumetric flask. Add 15 ml conc. HCL and make up to volume with distilled water.
- Stock Iodine Solution (0.1 N) - Place 12.7 g iodine in a 250 ml beaker, add 40 g potassium iodide and 25 ml water. Stir until all is dissolved, then dilute to 1 litre with distilled water.
- Iodine Solution (0.01 N) - Prepare approximately 0.01 N iodine solution by diluting 50 ml of stock solution to 500 ml with distilled water.
- Starch Indicator Solution - Triturate 0.4 gm soluble starch and 0.002 g mercuric iodide preservative with a little water and add the paste slowly to 200 ml boiling water. Continue boiling until the solution is clear, cool, and transfer to a glass-stoppered bottle.
- Potassium iodate
- Stock Sodium Thiosulfate Solution (0.1 N) - Prepare a stock solution by placing 25 g sodium thiosulfate pentahydrate in a beaker, add 0.1 g sodium carbonate and dissolve using boiled, cooled distilled water making the solution up to a final volume of 1 litre. Allow the solution to stand one day before standardizing.

To standardize, accurately weigh to the nearest 0.1 mg, 1.5 g primary standard potassium iodate dried at 180°C, dissolve, and dilute to volume in a 500 ml volumetric flask. Into a 500 ml Iodine flask, transfer 50 ml of iodate solution by pipette. Add 2 g potassium iodide and 10 ml of N hydrochloric acid and stopper the flask. After 5 min, titrate with stock thiosulfate solution to a pale yellow. Add 5 ml starch indicator solution and continue the titration until the blue colour disappears. Calculate the normality of the stock solution.

- Sodium Thiosulphate Titrant (0.01 N) - Dilute 100 ml of the stock thiosulfate solution to 1 litre with freshly boiled and cooled distilled water.
- Standardized Sulphite Solution for Preparation of Working SulphiteTCM Solution - Dissolve 0.30 g sodium metabisulphite ($Na_2S_2O_5$) or 0.40 g sodium sulphite (Na_2SO_3) in 500 ml of recently boiled, cooled, distilled water. Sulphite solution is unstable; it is, therefore, important to use water of the highest purity to minimize this instability. This solution contains the equivalent of 320-400 µg/ml of SO_2.
- Working Sulphite-TCM Solution - Measure 2 ml of the standard solution into a 100 ml volumetric flask by pipette and bring to mark with 0.04 M TCM. Calculate the concentration of sulphur dioxide in the working solution in micrograms of sulphur dioxide per millilitre. This solution is stable for 30 days if kept in the refrigerator at 5°C. If not kept at 5°C, prepare fresh daily.

SAMPLING

Place 30 ml of absorbing solution in an impinger and sample for four hours at the flow rate of 1 L/min. After sampling measure the volume of sample and transfer to a sample storage bottle.

ANALYSIS

Replace any water lost by evaporation during sampling by adding distilled water up to the calibration mark on the absorber. Mix thoroughly, pipette out 10 ml of the collected sample into a 25 ml

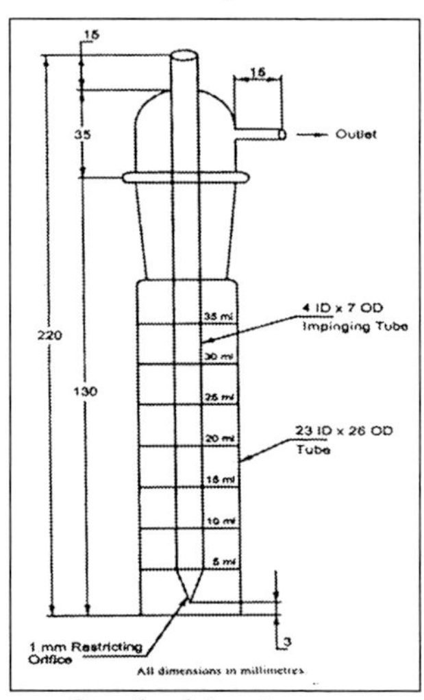

Standard Impinger

volumetric flask. Add 1 ml 0.6% sulphamic acid and allow reacting for 10 minutes to destroy the nitrite resulting from oxides of nitrogen. Add 2 ml of 0.2% formaldehyde solution and 2 ml pararosaniline solution and make up to 25 ml with distilled water. Prepare a blank in the same manner using 10 ml of unexposed absorbing reagent. After a 30 min colour development interval and before 60 minutes, measure and record the absorbance of samples and reagent blank at 560 nm. Use distilled water; not the reagent blank, as the optical reference.

CALIBRATION

The actual concentration of the sulphite solution is determined by adding excess iodine and back titrating with standard sodium thiosulfate solution. To back-titrate, measure, by pipette, 50 ml of the 0.01 N iodine solution into each of two 500 ml iodine flasks A and B. To flask A (blank) add 25 ml distilled water and into flask B (sample) measure 25 ml sulphite solution by pipette. Stopper the flasks and allow to react for 5 minutes. Prepare the working sulphite-TCM solution at the same time iodine solution is added to the flasks. By means of a burette containing standardized 0.01 N thiosulfate, titrate each flask in turn to a pale yellow. Then add 5 ml starch solution and continue the titration until the blue colour disappears.

Preparation of Standards

Measure 0.5 ml, 1.0 ml, 1.5 ml, 2.0 ml, 2.5 ml, 3.0 ml, 3.5 ml and 4.0 ml of working sulphite TCM solution in 25 ml volumetric flask. Add sufficient TCM solution to each flask to bring the volume to approximately 10 ml. Then add the remaining reagents as described in the procedure for analysis. A reagent blank with 10 ml absorbing solution is also prepared. Read the absorbance of each standard and reagent blank.

Standard Curve

Plot a curve absorbance (Y axis) versus concentration (X axis). Draw a line of best fit and determine the slope. The reciprocal of slope gives the calibration factor (CF).

CALCULATION

Concentration of sulphite solution:

$$C = \frac{(V1\text{-}V2) \times N \times K}{V}$$

Where,

$C = SO_2$ concentration in mg/ml

V1 = Volume of thiosulfate for blank, ml

V2 = Volume of thiosulfate for sample, ml

N = Normality of thiosulfate

K = 32000 (Milliequivalent weight $SO_2/\mu g$)

V = Volume of standard sulphite solution, ml

$C\ (SO_2\ \mu g/m^3) = (A_s - A_b) \times CF \times V_s/V_a \times V_t$

Where,

CSO_2 = Concentration of Nitrogen dioxide, $\mu g/m^3$

A_s = Absorbance of sample

A_b = Absorbance of reagent blank

CF = Calibration factor

V_a = Volume of air sampled, m^3

V_s = Volume of sample, ml

V_t = Volume of aliquot taken for analysis, ml

QUALITY CONTROL

Quality Control (QC) is the techniques that are used to fulfill requirements for quality. The QC procedures for the air sampling and monitoring sections of this protocol include preventative maintenance of equipment, calibration of equipment, analysis of field blanks and lab blanks.

IS 5182 Part 2 Method of Measurement of Air Pollution: Sulphur Dioxide

FLOW CHART FOR MEASUREMENT OF SULPHUR DIOXIDE
Place 30 ml of absorbing media in an impinger
Connect it to the gas-sampling manifold of gas sampling device (RDS/HVS).
Draw air at a sampling rate of 1 lpm for four hours
Check the volume of sample at the end of sampling and record it
Transfer the exposed samples in storage bottle and preserve
Prepare calibration graph as recommended in method
Take 10/20 ml. aliquot of sample in 25 ml. Vol. Flask
Take 10/20 ml. of unexposed sample in 25 ml. Vol. Flask (blank)
Add 1 ml Sulphamic acid. Keep it 10 minutes
Add 2 ml formaldehyde
Add 2 ml working PRA
Make up to mark (25 ml.) with distilled water.
Keep it 30 minutes for reaction
Set Zero of spectrophotometer with Distilled water
Measure absorbance at 560 nm
Calculate concentration using calibration graph
Calculate concentration of Sulphur Dioxide in $\mu g/m^3$

GUIDELINES FOR SAMPLING AND ANALYSIS OF NITROGEN DIOXIDE IN AMBIENT AIR (MODIFIED JACOB AND HOCHHEISER METHOD)

PURPOSE

The purpose of this protocol is to provide guidelines for monitoring of nitrogen dioxide in ambient.

STANDARD

The national ambient air quality standard for nitrogen dioxide is presented in the table:

Pollutant	Time Weighted Average	Concentration in Ambient Air	
		Industrial, Residential, Rural and other Areas	Ecologically Sensitive Area (Notified by Central Government)
Nitrogen dioxide (NO_2), $\mu g/m^3$	Annual* 24 Hours**	40 80	30 80

* Annual Arithmetic mean of minimum 104 measurements in a year at a particular site taken twice a week 24 hourly at uniform intervals.

** 24 hourly or 8 hourly or 1 hourly monitored values, as applicable, shall be complied with 98% of the time in a year. 2% of the time, they may exceed the limits but not on two consecutive days of monitoring.

PRINCIPLE OF THE METHOD

Modified Jacobs & Hochheiser Method (IS 5182 Part 6 Methods for Measurement of Air Pollution: Oxides of nitrogen).

Ambient nitrogen dioxide (NO_2) is collected by bubbling air through a solution of sodium hydroxide and sodium arsenite. The concentration of nitrite ion (NO^-_2) produced during sampling is determined colorimetrically by reacting the nitrite ion with phosphoric acid, sulfanilamide, and N-(1-naphthyl)ethylenediamine di-hydrochloride (NEDA) and measuring the absorbance of the highly coloured azo-dye at 540 n m.

INSTRUMENT/EQUIPMENT

The following items are necessary to perform the monitoring and analysis of nitrogen dioxide in ambient air:

- Analytical balance
- Vacuum pump: Capable of maintaining a vacuum of at least 0.6 atmospheres across the flow control device. Flow control device capable of maintaining a constant flow of 200-1000 ml per minute through the sampling solution
- Calibrated flow measuring device: To control the airflow from 0.2 to 1 l/min.
- Absorber: a midget impinger
- Spectrophotometer: Capable of measuring absorbance at 540 nm equipped with 1 cm path length cells.
- Glass wares: low actinic glassware must be used for analysis

REAGENTS/CHEMICALS

All the chemicals should meet specifications of ACS Analytical Reagent grade

- Distilled water
- Sodium hydroxide
- Sodium Arsenite
- Absorbing solution (Dissolve 4.0 g of sodium hydroxide in distilled water, add 1.0 g of sodium Arsenite, and dilute to 1,000 ml with distilled water)
- Sulphanilamide - Melting point 165 to 167°C
- N-(1-Naphthyl)-ethylenediamine Di-hydrochloride (NEDA) - A 1% aqueous solution should have only one absorption peak at 320 nm over the range of 260-400 nm. NEDA showing more than one absorption peak over this range is impure and should not be used
- Hydrogen Peroxide - 30%
- Phosphoric Acid - 85%
- Sulphanilamide Solution - Dissolve 20 g of sulphanilamide in 700 ml of distilled water. Add, with mixing, 50 ml of

85% phosphoric acid and dilute to 1,000 ml. This solution is stable for one month, if refrigerated

- NEDA Solution - Dissolve 0.5 g of NEDA in 500 ml of distilled water. This solution is stable for one month, if refrigerated and protected from light.
- Hydrogen Peroxide Solution - Dilute 0.2 ml of 30% hydrogen peroxide to 250 ml with distilled water. This solution may be used for one month, if, refrigerated and protected from light
- Sodium nitrite - Assay of 97% $NaNO_2$ or greater
- Sodium Nitrite stock solution (1000 µg NO_2/ml)
- Sodium Nitrite solution (10 µg NO_2/ml.)
- Sodium Nitrite working solution (1 µg NO_2/ml)

  (Dilute with absorbing reagent, prepare fresh daily)

SAMPLING

Place 30 ml of absorbing solution in an impinger and sample for four hour at the flow rate of 0.2 to 1 L/min. After sampling measure the volume of sample and transfer to a sample storage bottle.

ANALYSIS

Replace any water lost by evaporation during sampling by adding distilled water up to the calibration mark on the absorber, mix thoroughly.

Pipette out 10 ml of the collected sample into a 50 ml volumetric flask. Pipette in 1 ml of hydrogen peroxide solution, 10 ml of sulphanilamide solution, and 1.4 ml of NEDA solution, with thorough mixing after the addition of each reagent and make up to 50 ml with distilled water.

Prepare a blank in the same manner using 10 ml of unexposed absorbing reagent.

After a 10 min colour development interval, measure and record the absorbance of samples and reagent blank at 540 nm.

Use distilled water; not the reagent blank, as the optical reference.

Samples with an absorbance greater than 1.0 must be re-analyzed after diluting an aliquot of the collected samples with an equal quantity of unexposed absorbing reagent.

A randomly selected 5-10% of the samples should be re-analyzed as apart of an internal quality assurance program.

CALIBRATION

Preparation of Standards

Pipette 1, 2, 3, 4, 5, 6, 7, 8, 9, 10, 12, 15 and 20 ml of working standard solution in to 50 ml volumetric flask. Fill to 20 ml mark with absorbing solution. A reagent blank with 10 ml absorbing solution is also prepared. Add reagents to each volumetric flask as in the procedure for analysis. Read the absorbance of each standard and reagent blank against distilled water reference.

Standard Curve

Plot a curve absorbance (Y axis) versus concentration (X axis). Draw a line of best fit and determine the slope. The reciprocal of slope gives the calibration factor (CF).

CALCULATION

$$C\,(NO_2\ \mu g/m^3) = (A_s - A_b) \times CF \times V_s/V_a \times V_t \times 0.82$$

Where,

$C\ NO_2$ = Concentration of Nitrogen dioxide, $\mu g/m^3$

A_s = Absorbance of sample

A_b = Absorbance of reagent blank

CF = Calibration factor

V_a = Volume of air sampled, m^3

V_s = Volume of sample, ml

V_t = Volume of aliquot taken for analysis, ml

0.82 = Sampling efficiency

QUALITY CONTROL

Quality Control (QC) is the techniques that are used to fulfil requirements for quality. The QC procedures for the air sampling and monitoring sections of this protocol include preventative maintenance of equipment, calibration of equipment, analysis of field blanks and lab blanks.

FLOW CHART FOR MEASUREMENT OF NITROGEN DIOXIDE
Place 30 ml of absorbing media in an impinger
Connect it to the gas sampling manifold of gas sampling device (RDS/HVS).
Draw air at a sampling rate of 1 lpm for four hours
Check the volume of sample at the end of sampling and record it
Transfer the exposed samples in storage bottle and preserve
Prepare calibration graph as recommended in method
Take 10 ml. aliquot of sample in 50 ml. Vol. Flask
Take 10 ml. of unexposed sample in 50 ml. Vol. Flask (blank)
Add 1 ml hydrogen peroxide
Add 10 ml sulphanilamide
Add 1.4 ml NEDA
Make up to mark (50 ml.) with distilled water
Keep it 10 minutes for reaction
Set Zero of spectrophotometer with Distilled water
Measure absorbance at 540 nm
Calculate concentration using calibration graph
Calculate concentration of Nitrogen Dioxide in $\mu g/m^3$

GUIDELINES FOR SAMPLING AND ANALYSIS OF PARTICULATE MATTER (PM_{10}) IN AMBIENT AIR (GRAVIMETRIC METHOD)

PURPOSE

The purpose of this protocol is to provide guidelines for monitoring and analysis of Particulate Matter PM_{10} in ambient air.

STANDARD

The national ambient air quality standards for Particulate Matter PM_{10} is presented in the table:

Pollutant	Time Weighted Average	Concentration in Ambient Air	
		Industrial, Residential, Rural and other Areas	Ecologically Sensitive Area (Notified by Central Government)
Particulate Matter, PM10, µg/m^3	Annual* 24 Hours**	60 100	60 100

* Annual Arithmetic mean of minimum 104 measurements in a year at a particular site taken twice a week 24 hourly at uniform intervals.

** 24 hourly or 8 hourly or 1 hourly monitored values, as applicable, shall be complied with 98% of the time in a year. 2% of the time, they may exceed the limits but not on two consecutive days of monitoring.

PRINCIPLE OF THE METHOD

Air is drawn through a size-selective inlet and through a 20.3 × 25.4 cm (8 × 10 in) filter at a flow rate, which is typically 1132 L/min. Particles with aerodynamic diameter less than the cut-point of the inlet are collected, by the filter. The mass of these particles is determined by the difference in filter weights prior to and after sampling. The concentration of PM_{10} in the designated size range is calculated by dividing the weight gain of the filter by the volume of air sampled.

INSTRUMENT/EQUIPMENT

The following items are necessary to perform the monitoring and analysis of Particulate Matter PM_{10} in ambient air:

- Analytical balance:
- Sampler: High Volume Sampler with size selective inlet for PM_{10} and automatic volumetric flow control
- Calibrated flow-measuring device to control the airflow at 1132 l/min.
- Top loading orifice kit

Reagents/Chemicals

Filter Media – A Glass fibre filter of 20.3 × 25.4 cm (8 × 10 in) size

SAMPLING

Field Sampling - Tilt back the inlet and secure it according to manufacturer's instructions. Loosen the faceplate wing nuts and remove the faceplate. Remove the filter from its jacket and centre it on the support screen with the rough side of the filter facing upwards. Replace the faceplate and tighten the wing nuts to secure the rubber gasket against the filter edge. Gently lower the inlet. For automatically flow-controlled units, record the designated flow rate on the data sheet. Record the reading of the elapsed time meter. The specified length of sampling is commonly 8 hours or 24 hours. During this period, several reading (hourly) of flow rate should be taken.

After the required time of sampling, record the flow meter reading, take out the filter media from the sampler, and put in a container or envelope.

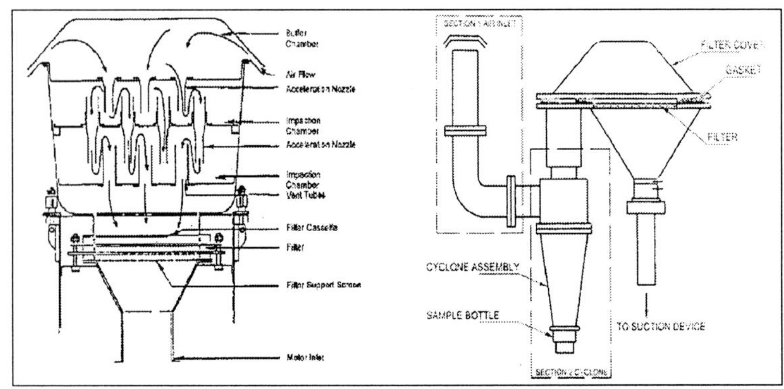

PM_{10} Sampler (Impaction Inlet) PM_{10} Sampler (Cyclonic Inlet)

ANALYSIS

Filter inspection: Inspect the filter for pin holes using a light table. Loose particles should be removed with a soft brush. Apply the filter identification number or a code to the filter if it is not a numbered. Condition the filter in conditioning room maintained within 20-30 C and 40-50% relative humidity or in an airtight desiccator for 24 hours. Take initial weight of the filter paper (Wi) before sampling. Condition the filter after sampling in conditioning room maintained within 20-30 C and 40-50% relative humidity or in an airtight desiccator for 24 hours. Take final weight of the filter paper (Wf)

CALIBRATION

Periodical calibration of the sampler is being done by Orifice Transfer Standard - The PM_{10} sampler calibration orifice consists of a 3.175 cm (1.25 in) diameter hole in the end cap of 7.62 cm (3 in) diameter by 20.3 cm (8 in) long hollow metal cylinder. This orifice is mounted tightly to the filter support in place of the inlet during calibration.

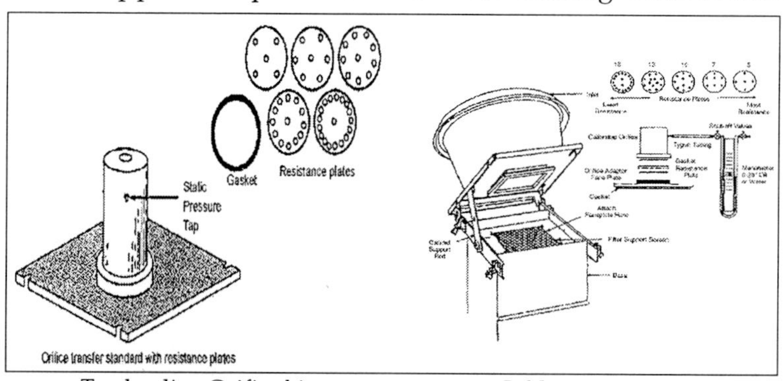

Top loading Orifice kit   Calibration set up

A small tap on the side of the cylinder is provided to measure the pressure drop across the orifice. A flow rate of 1132 L/min through the orifice typically results in a pressure difference of several inches of water. The relationship between pressure difference and flow rate is established via a calibration curve derived from measurements against a primary standard such as a Roots meter at standard temperature and pressure. Flow resistances that simulate filter resistances are introduced at the end of the calibrator opposite the orifice by a set of perforated circular disks.

CALCULATION

C PM10 μg/m^3 = (Wf – Wi) × 106/V

Where,

C PM_{10} = Concentration of Nitrogen dioxide, μg/m^3

Wf = Initial weight of filter in g

Wi = Initial weight of filter in g

106 = Conversion of g to μg

V = Volume of air sampled, m3

QUALITY CONTROL

Quality Control (QC) is the techniques that are used to fulfill requirements for quality. The QC procedures for the air sampling and monitoring sections of this protocol include preventative maintenance of equipment, calibration of equipment, analysis of field blanks and lab blanks.

FLOW CHART FOR MEASUREMENT OF PM_{10}
Check the filter for any physical damages
Mark identification number on the filter
Condition the filter in conditioning room/desiccator for 24 hours
Record initial weight
Place the filter on the sampler
Run the sampler for eight hours
Record the flow rate on hourly basis
Remove the filter from the sampler

(Contd...)

Keep the exposed filter in a proper container
Record the total time of sampling & average flow rate
Again condition the filter in conditioning room/desiccator for 24 hours
Record final weight
Calculate the concentration of PM_{10} in µg/m^3

GUIDELINES FOR DETERMINATION OF $PM_{2.5}$ IN AMBIENT AIR (GRAVIMETRIC METHOD)

PURPOSE

The purpose of this protocol is to provide guidelines for monitoring and analysis of Particulate Matter $PM_{2.5}$ in ambient air.

DEFINITION

$PM_{2.5}$ refers to fine particles that are 2.5 micrometers (µm) or smaller in diameter. Ambient air is defined as any unconfined part of the Earth's atmosphere, that the surrounding outdoor air in which humans and other organisms live and breathe. FRM – Federal Reference Method

FEM – Federal Equivalent Method

STANDARD

Pollutant	Time Weighted Average	Concentration in Ambient Air	
		Industrial, Residential, Rural and other Areas	Ecologically Sensitive Area (Notified by Central Government)
Particulate Matter, $PM_{2.5}$, µg/m^3	Annual* 24 Hours**	40 60	40 60

* Annual Arithmetic mean of minimum 104 measurements in a year at a particular site taken twice a week 24 hourly at uniform intervals.

** 24 hourly or 8 hourly or 1 hourly monitored values, as applicable, shall be complied with 98% of the time in a year. 2% of the time, they may exceed the limits but not on two consecutive days of monitoring.

PRINCIPLE

An electrically powered air sampler draws ambient air at a constant volumetric flow rate (16.7 lpm) maintained by a mass flow/volumetric flow controller coupled to a microprocessor into specially designed inertial particle-size separator (i.e. cyclones or impactors) where the suspended particulate matter in the PM2.5 size ranges is separated for collection on a 47 mm polytetrafluoroethylene (PTFE) filter over a specified sampling period. Each filter is weighed before and after sample collection to determine the net gain due to the particulate matter. The mass concentration in the ambient air is computed as the total mass of collected particles in the PM2.5 size ranges divided by the actual volume of air sampled, and is expressed in $\mu g/m^3$. The microprocessor reads averages and stores five-minute averages of ambient temperature, ambient pressure, filter temperature and volumetric flow rate. In addition, the microprocessor calculates the average temperatures and pressure, total volumetric flow for the entire sample run time and the coefficient of variation of the flow rate.

INTERFERENCES AND ARTEFACTS

The potential effect of body moisture or oils contacting the filters is minimized by using non-serrated forceps to handle the filters at all times. This measure also moderates interference due to static electricity.

Teflon filters accumulate a surface electrical charge, which may affect filter weight. Static electricity is controlled by treating filters with a "Static Master" static charge neutralizer prior to weighing. Placement of filters on a "Static Master" unit is required for a minimum of 30 seconds before any filter can be weighed.

Moisture content can affect filter weight. Filters must be equilibrated for a minimum of 24 hours in a controlled environment prior to pre- and postweighing. The balance room's relative humidity must be maintained at a mean value range of 45 ± 5% and its air temperature must be maintained at a mean value range of 25.0 ± °C.

Airborne particulate can adversely affect accurate mass measurement of the filter. Filters undergoing conditioning should not be placed within an airflow path created by air conditioning ductwork, computer printers, or frequently opened doorways. Cleaning laboratory bench-tops and weighing areas daily, installing "sticky" floor mats at doorway entrances to the balance room and wearing clean lab coats over regular clothing can further minimize dust contamination.

PRECISION AND ACCURACY

The performance segment of the $PM_{2.5}$ FRM specifies strict guidelines for controls that must be observed, as well as the range of precision and accuracy of those controls. The flow rate through the instrument is specified as 16.67 lpm (1 m^3/hr). This flow must be volumetrically controlled to a precision of 5% and an accuracy of 2%. The flow control must be upgraded at least every 30 seconds and recorded (logged) every five minutes. Barometric pressure, ambient temperature and filter temperature should be measured on the same schedule. Filter temperature, it must not exceed the ambient temperature by more than 5° C for more than 30 minutes. A fan blowing filtered ambient air through the enclosure provides the necessary cooling effect. It is necessary for the entire apparatus to provide accurate performance over a temperature range of –20 to 50° C. The supporting run-time (interval) data, which are stored in detailed 5 minute intervals in the sampler's microprocessor, as well as 24-hour integrated performance (filter) data, must be capable of being extracted at the completion of a 24-hour run. The FRM mandates the provision of an RS232 port for this purpose. Data may be extracted to a portable computer.

Mass of the filter deposit, flow rate through the filter, and sampling time have typical precision of ± 0.2 mg, ± 5%, and ± 30 seconds, respectively. These uncertainties combine to yield a propagated precision of approximately ± 5 % at 10 μg/m3 and approximately ± 2% at 100 $\mu g/m^3$.

SITTING REQUIREMENTS

Samplers should be sited to meet the goals of the specific monitoring project. For routine sampling to determine compliance with the National Ambient Air Quality Standards (NAAQS), sampler sitting is described in CPCB guidelines shall apply.

The monitoring should be done at outside the zone of influence of sources located within the designated zone of representation for the monitoring site. Height of the inlet must be 3-10 m above the ground level. And at a suitable distance from any direct pollution source including traffic.

Large nearby buildings and trees extending above the height of the monitor may present barriers or deposition surfaces for PM. Distance of the sampler to any air flow obstacle i.e. buildings, must be more than two times the height of the obstacle above the sampler.

There should be unrestricted airflow in three of four quadrants.

Certain trees may also be sources of PM in the form of detritus, pollen, or insect parts. These can be avoided by locating samplers by placing them > 20 m from nearby trees.

If collocated sampling has to be performed the minimum distance between two Samplers should be 2 m.

APPARATUS AND MATERIALS

- Sampling equipment designated as FRM (Federal Reference Method) or FEM (Federal Equivalent Method)
- Certified Flow Transfer Standard for Flow Calibration

  Following established EPA methods and procedures, all calibration transfer standards (i.e. temperature, pressure and flow) must be certified against traceable standards at least once per year. Calibration of these transfer standards will be conducted by the transfer standard manufacturer.
- Certified Standards for Pressure and Temperature (Optional)

- Electronic microbalance with a minimum resolution of 0.001 mg and a precision of ± 0.001 mg, supplied with a balance pan. The microbalance must be positioned on a vibration-damping balance support table.
- Calibration weights, utilized as Mass Reference Standards, should be non-corroding, range in weight from 100 mg to 200 mg, and be certified as traceable to NIST mass standards. The weights should be ASTM Class 1 category with a tolerance of 0.025 mg.
- Non-serrated forceps for handling filters.
- Non-metallic, non-serrated forceps for handling weights.
- Digital timer/stopwatch.
- 47 mm Filter: Teflon membrane, 46.2 mm effective diameter with a polypropylene support ring or filters as recommended by FRM/FEM sampler manufacturer.
- Filter support cassettes and covers.
- Filter equilibration racks.
- Relative Humidity/Temperature recorder.
- NIST-certified or ISO traceable Hygrometer for calibration of relative humidity readings.
- NIST-certified ISO traceable Thermometer for calibration of temperature readings.
- Light box.
- Radioactive (alpha particle) Polonium-210 ("Static Master") antistatic strips for static charge neutralization however static charge gives lowmoderate interference in stability of reading of balance.
- Antistatic, nitrate-free, phosphate-free, sulphate-free, and powder free vinyl gloves.
- Plastic petri-slide filters containers (Filter Cassette).
- Zip-lock plastic bags, 6"×9".
- Disposable laboratory wipes.
- Filter equilibration cabinets.
- Impactor oil/grease

SAMPLING AND ANALYTICAL PROCEDURE

Calibration and performance check of Sampler

External Leak Check

Upon initial installation of the sampler, following sampler repair or maintenance and at least monthly, perform a sampler external leak check according to the manufacturer's guidelines.

Internal Leak Check

Upon initial installation of the sampler, following sampler repair or maintenance, and at least monthly, perform a sampler internal leak check according to the manufacturer's guidelines.

Single-point Ambient Temperature and Filter Temperature

Verification Check

A single-point temperature verification check of both the ambient temperature and filter temperature sensors must be performed at least once every month. The Temperature check is performed following manufacturer's guidelines.

Ambient Temperature Calibration

The ambient temperature calibration is to be performed upon initial installation, yearly after site installation after any major maintenance that might affect the temperature reading, and at any time thereafter when the sampler fails a verification check following manufacturer's guidelines.

Filter Temperature Calibration

The filter temperature calibration is to be performed upon initial installation, yearly after site installation, and at any time thereafter when the sampler fails either a single-point or multi-point temperature verification check. To perform the temperature calibrations of filter follow the manufacturer's instructions.

Pressure Verification Check

Single-point pressure verification must be performed at least once every month. The pressure check is performed following manufacturer's instructions.

Pressure Calibration

The pressure calibration is to be performed upon initial installation, yearly after site installation, and at any time thereafter when the sampler fails a single-point pressure verification check. Pressure calibration shall be performed following manufacturer's instructions.

Single-point Flow Verification Check

A single-point flow verification check must be performed at least every month. The flow check is performed following manufacturer's instructions.

Multi-Point Flow Calibration Procedure

A multi-point flow calibration must be performed upon initial installation and once per year thereafter. In addition, the multi-point calibration must be performed whenever a single-point flow verification check indicates that the sampler flow deviates from the flow transfer standard by more than ± 4%. The multi-point calibration is performed following manufacturer's instructions.

Selection and Procurement of Filters

The quality of filter papers to be used should technically meet the desired specifications. It is preferable to prepare the estimate for whole requirement and order the same in bulk with a request to supply the same batch/lot of filters to control analytical quality and blank values. During the selection of filters following points should be considered:

- Mechanical stability;
- Chemical stability;
- Particle or gas sampling efficiency;
- Flow resistance;
- Loading capacity;
- Blank values;
- Artefact formation;
- Compatibility with analysis method; and
- Cost and availability.

47 mm (diameter) Teflon (PTFE) filter paper with Polypropylene support ring manufactured by M/s Whatman or M/s Pall Life Sciences or equivalent having 2 μm pore sizes. The filter papers should have very low background concentrations for ion and elements.

Filter Inspection and Conditioning of Filter Papers

Filter papers selected for different analytical objectives should be conditioned by following steps:

- Inspect all the filter papers for holes or cracks. Reject, if any deformity is found.
- Note down the batch/lot in log sheet.
- Label all the filters following a general lab coding technique, which should be unique to represent a sample.
- Put the marked filters in petri dishes.
- Use always proper (blunt) tweezers/forceps (made of non-reactive material) to handle the filter papers in lab and field as well.
- Prepare a sample-tracking sheet for each filter paper or a batch of filter paper.

Filter Inspection and Stability

To equilibrate, the filters are transferred from their sealed manufacturer's packaging to a filter-handling container such as a plastic petri-slide. The filters are handled with non-serrated forceps. Lab personnel must wear vinyl gloves as secondary when filters are being prepared for conditioning and weighing. Before any filter is placed in a filter-handling container, it must be inspected for defects. This is done be an examination of the filter on a "light table". A filter must be discarded if any defects are identified. Specific defects to look for are:

- Pinhole – A small hole appearing as a distinct and obvious bright point of light when examined over a light table.
- Separation of ring – Any separation or lack of seal between the filter and the filter support ring.
- Chaff or flashing – Any extra material on the reinforcing ring or on the heat-seal area that would prevent an airtight seal during sampling.

- Loose materials – Any extra loose materials or dirt particles on the filter.
- Discoloration – Any obvious discoloration that might be evidence of contamination.
- Other – A filter with any imperfection not described above, such as irregular surfaces or other results of poor workmanship.

Filter Conditioning

A one-month storage period in a controlled environment, followed by one week equilibration in the weighing environment, found acceptable deviations in reweighing. Gravimetric measurement is the net mass on a filter by weighing the filter before and after sampling with a balance in a temperature and relative humidity controlled environment as described in SOPs. To minimize particle volatilization and aerosol liquid water bias, $PM_{2.5}$ reference methods require that filters be equilibrated for 24 hours at a constant (within ±5%) relative humidity 45% and at a constant (within ±2°C) temperature between 25°C. These filter equilibrium conditions are intended to minimize the liquid water associated with soluble compounds and to minimize the loss of volatile species.

Lot Blanks Check

Randomly select three filters as lot blanks from each new lot received and place in individual containers. Equilibrate the exposed filters in a filter equilibration cabinet in the Balance Room that allows air circulation, but still reduces extraneous airborne particles from settling on filters. Weigh lot blanks every 24 hours on a designated balance.

Record the lot number, filter number, mass, and dates of the lot blanks in the assigned quality control logbook. Once the mass difference between weighing is less than 0.015 mg for all three lot blanks, the filters have stabilized. Note the time taken from initial exposure of the filters to attainment of mass stability. This information is designated as the minimum equilibration period required before filters from the same lot can be pre-weighed and used for routine sampling. Once this minimum equilibration period is determined, the lot blanks become lab blanks which are set aside for long-term exposure in the same equilibration cabinet where routine samples, field blanks, and trip blanks are equilibrated prior to pre- or post-weighing.

Laboratory Conditions for Weighing

Gravimetric analysis of the filters needs to be performed with a microbalance. The sensitivity and reliability of the electro-balance is about + 0.001 mg or 1 µg. Though tolerances on re-weights of Teflonmembrane filters are typically ± 0.010 mg, these sensitive balances require isolation from vibration and air currents. Balances placed in laminar flow hoods with filtered air minimize contamination of filters from particles and gases in laboratory air. Electrostatic effects contribute another main interference in gravimetric analysis of filters. It is established that residual charge on a filter could produce an electrostatic discharge between the filter on the pan and the metal casing of the electro balance, which induces non-gravimetric forces. This charge can be removed from most filter media by exposing the filter to a low-level radioactive source (500 Pico curies of polonium210) prior to and during sample weighing.

Electro Balance Controls and Calibration

Gravimetric mass analysis is performed using single pan electronic balance. If possible, polonium strip ionization units are used to reduce electrostatic effects in the weighing cavity and on individual filters. A segregated laboratory area is used to control human traffic and to stabilize the temperature and relative humidity of the weighing environment. The area is cleaned with a high efficiency vacuum cleaner, and a tacky floor covering is installed at the entrance to the sample handling room to minimize dust artifact. Gravimetric analysis of filters currently uses the difference method to determine the mass of the collected aerosol. The pre weight of each filter is measured prior to being sent into the field for sampling.

Once exposed and returned to the sample handling room, the filter is removed petri dishes and the post weight of the filter is measured after conditioning. The mass of the aerosol is determined by calculating the difference between the pre and post weights.

Cleaning and Maintenance of the Sample Handling Room

The requirements for a sample handling room include a reduced dust environment, and, over the twenty-four hour period prior to analysis of exposed filters, temperature in the range of 25° C with variation less than ± 3° C, and relative humidity 45% ±5%. Every last working day, the sample handling room should be thoroughly cleaned, after insuring that all filters have been protected against contamination. To reduce fugitive dust levels, all surfaces are cleaned with a high efficiency vacuum. The floors are cleaned with a mild cleaning solution, if necessary. Finally, all work surfaces are cleaned with reagent grade alcohol (or another reagent grade solvent, if necessary) and Kimwipes™. This procedure reduces the possibility of contamination if a filter falls to the work surface. Following the Friday cleaning, no analysis shall occur for at least twenty-four hours to reduce the potential for contamination of filters by compounds used in the cleaning process.

Calibration and Maintenance of balance

The balance is cleaned and calibrated every day for ranges at the start of operation. It is also recalibrated if the balance fails a "zero" test that is performed periodically. A calibration log database is maintained for each balance. Significant events concerning the balance and any balance maintenance other than routine procedures are recorded in the log of the lab manager.

Cleaning

Regular cleaning should be performed as following:

- Clean the metal and plastic forceps with ethanol and a Kimwipe™.

- Clean the work surface around the balance with ethanol and a Kimwipe™.
- Clean the top surface and the strips of the anti static ionizing units by gently rubbing with a Kimwipe™ wetted with ethanol. Do not neglect to clean the ionizing unit in the electro balance.
- Replace the clean ionizing unit in the center back of the balance cavity, and close the door on the weighing chamber (if polonium strip is used).

Thorough Calibration of Balance (Once in 6 Months)

- Allow the balance to stabilize with no weights on the pan. The computer will automatically record the mass to the screen when the balance has stabilized; this is the "zero" mass. It should be within 0.010 mg of 0.000. If not, contact the lab manager (see step 3, section 4.3.2.1 for lab manager procedures).
- Set the zero on the balance by pressing the tare button on the balance. This forces the "zero" mass to be exactly 0.000.
- Calibrate the balance. Momentarily ground yourself by touching the balance casing. Use nylon forceps to remove the certified calibration weight from its container. Gently place it in the center and allow the mass reading to stabilize and stop decreasing. Take readings.
- Use a 200.000 mg or suitable mass of graded Calibration weight.
- Use a 20.000 mg or suitable mass graded Calibration weight.
- Remove the calibration weight from the bail, using the nylon forceps, and replace it in its storage container.
- Check the calibration of the balance using the test weight. Momentarily ground yourself by touching the balance casing. Use the nylon forceps to remove the test weight from its container.
- Place the test weight in the center of the balance pan and allow the mass reading to stabilize and stop

decreasing. The computer will record a reading to the screen when the balance has stabilized. The test weight is an old 50.000 gm calibration weight.

- Allow the balance to return to "zero." Compare the zero value and the value determined for the 50.000 mg mass to the expected values posted on the balance. If they exceed 02 micrograms, repeat the procedure. If variations greater than 10 micrograms are observed, report to the laboratory manager so that he/she can take appropriate action (section 4.3.2.1 step 3).
- On a random basis, but at least semiannually, the laboratory supervisor shall request a comparison of the normal calibration standards with a master set of reference standard masses maintained by the laboratory supervisor. After calibration, measure these 200.000, 50.000, and 20.000 mg standards and report their masses to the supervisor. The results are used to verify the integrity of the electro balance and the standard masses used in daily calibrations.
- The electro balance is available to run controls or for routine determination of mass.
- Linearity checks (Once in a year otherwise after every repair/shifting of balance). To run a linearity check on the balance (if the balance is suspected to be damaged), utilize the series of four standard weights stored in the lab manager's desk. The four weights, 200 mg, 100 mg, 50 mg, and 20 mg, must be weighed and a regression line developed. Take following steps for performing Linearity checks:
- Use the nylon forceps to remove a weight from its container and place it on the weighing pan.
- Wait until the balance has stabilized (approximately one minute). Then, record the displayed weight as the 'y' value and the certified mass as the 'x' value.
- Remove the weight from the pan, using the plastic forceps, and replace it in its protective container.
- Repeat steps (i) through (iii) for the other three weights.

- Linearly regress the 'y' value versus the 'x' value. Calculate the r^2 value.
- If the R^2 is not better than 0.995, the balance requires maintenance.

Stability Check of Balance (Once in Month)

To check the stability of the balance, reweigh the last 20 archived control filters, and develop a regression line comparing the re-weight values to the original values. Use following steps:

- Reweigh the series of 20 old controls filters on the suspect balance.
- Plot the re-weights versus the original weights.
- Derive the best line fit equation correlating the original weights to the reweights.
- Calculate the standard deviation and the r^2 of the line fit.
- If the standard deviation is greater than ±3 micrograms, and the r^2 is not better than 0.995, the balance should be carefully inspected and submitted for maintenance.

Daily Calibration of Balance

Internal Calibration should be performed daily before any Pre- or Postsampling weighing.

Internal Calibration

Open the draft shield door for at least one minute to allow the balanceweighing chamber to equilibrate to room temperature, then, close the draft shield door.

Press the "TARE" key when readout has stabilized to ensure zero-readout. The liquid crystal display (LCD) should display "0.000 mg". Press the key for ensuring the internal calibration.

External Calibration

Open the draft shield door. Place a 100 mg working reference standard calibration weight onto the microbalance pan with non-metallic forceps. Close the draft shield door.

Record the date, temperature and relative humidity of the balance room, and mass readout in the quality control logbook assigned to the microbalance. Remove the calibration weight and tare the microbalance as described above. Enter the calibration data into logbook records and assign to the calibration session in the quality control logbook assigned to the microbalance. External calibration must be performed for each day on which filters are pre-weighed and/or postweighed.

Weighing of Filters

- Take out pre-conditioned filters by forceps one by one and weigh properly. Record the mass in data sheet and log books against respective filter numbers or code. Always use gloved hands and blunt tweezers to handle filters.
- Replace and close the filter container (Petri dishes). Weigh one Control Filters (Archived one) with each batch of ten weighing. Keep separate controls for Pre (Blank filter) and Post (Exposed) sampling filters.
- Put the values of all control measurement in Quality Control Charts against dates.
- Put Lab code on from Plastic petri-slide filter containers (Filter Cassette).
- Take out conditioned filter from Plastic petri-slide filter containers (Filter Cassette).
    - Weigh the preconditioned filter. o Record and store it in laboratory coded filter cassette.
- Follow the same procedure for exposed filter
- Place the weighed filter into a petri-slide, close tightly, and store at 4°C for at least one year after sampling.

Shipment of Pre-weighed filters

Put the marked pre-weighed filters in Zip pouch. Transport the filters in a dry clean box (temperature control is optional) to the field.

Field sampling

- On the Field Data Log, fill in the top portion of the form including: the date/time of visit, the site identification, sampler identification, site name, filter ID number, sample start and stop dates and times, and field operator initials.
- Perform all necessary pre-sampling procedures as described above.
- Perform QA/QC checks or maintenance, if required.
- Record all maintenance activities in the field log book; include time, date, and any concerns that might affect the quality of the sample.
- Remove the filter to be installed from its protective filter cassette carrier.
- Fix the filter following manufacturer's instructions into place against the bottom of the WINS impactor.
- Check the system clock and make sure it is within 1 min of NIST time.
- Strictly follow operator's manual for setting up the sampling programme (24 hours)
- The Filter Setup Screen shows the start date and time and the end date and time for the next sample. To change the sampling parameters follow the operator's manual.
- Start Sampling run.
- Wait until the auto diagnosis for all relevant parameters finishes and the sampler automatically switch over to SAMPLING mode. Check flow (16.7LPM) and Sample volume displays rightly on screen.

Recovering the Sample and Data from a Completed Sample Run

- From the Main Screen, note the current sampler-operating mode (top line, right side of display). If the sampler is in the WAIT mode or the SAMP (sampling) mode, the sampler has not completed the previously scheduled sampling run. Do not disturb the sampler unless necessary.

- If the sampler is in the DONE mode or the ERR mode, press STOP. This allows the sampler to write the final information into storage for the current sample run and must be performed prior to filter exchange. The sampler mode should now indicate STOP.
- Open the filter exchange mechanism by pulling straight back on the black handle. The filter holder will lower away from the WINS impactor.
- Remove the filter carrier from the filter holder.
- Place the filter carrier in the filter cassette case.
- From the Main Screen, access to the Filter Data screen following operator's instruction.
- Using the information displayed on the Filter Data screen, complete the Field Data Log with the following information from the completed sample run:
  (a) Total Sample Volume – from the Vol. field
  (b) Average Flow Rate – from the Ave. Flow field
  (c) Coefficient of Variation – from the %CV field
  (d) Total Run Time – from the Tot field
  (e) Maximum Temperature Difference – from the Temp Diff field
  (f) Minimum, Average and Maximum Ambient Temperatures – from the AmbT fields
  (g) Minimum, Average and Maximum Filter Temperatures – from the FltT fields
  (h) Minimum, Average and Maximum Pressures – from the Pres fields
  (i) If the sampler indicated there was an error, note the error in the field log book and make any repairs as needed. Any fixes should be done prior to the next run date.

Calculation and Reporting of Mass Concentrations

The equation to calculate the mass of fine particulate matter collected on a Teflon filter is as below:

$M_{2.5} = (Mf - Mi)\ mg \times 10^3\ \mu g$

Where,

$M_{2.5}$ = total mass of fine particulate collected during sampling period (µg)

Mf = final mass of the conditioned filter after sample collection (mg) Mi = initial mass of the conditioned filter before sample collection (mg)

10^3 = unit conversion factor for milligrams (mg) to micrograms (µg)

- Field records of $PM_{2.5}$ samplers are required to provide measurements of the total volume of ambient air passing through the sampler (V) in cubic meters at the actual temperatures and pressures measured during sampling. Use the following formula if V is not available directly from the sampler:

  $$V = Qavg \times t \times 10^{-3}\ m^3$$

Where,

V = total sample value (m^3)

Qavg = average flow rate over the entire duration of the sampling period (L/min)

t = duration of sampling period (min)

10^3 = unit conversion factor for liters (L) into cubic meters (m^3)

The equation given below can be used to determine $PM_{2.5}$ mass concentration:

$$PM_{2.5} = M2.5/V$$

Where,

$PM_{2.5}$ = mass concentration of $PM_{2.5}$ particulates (µg/m^3)
$PM_{2.5}$ = total mass of fine particulate collected during sampling period (µg)

V = total volume of air sampled (m^3)

REPORTING

Data reporting should be done in prescribed Format. The Format shall contain all information including calibration. The data sheet must be accompanied by Sample Tracking sheet.

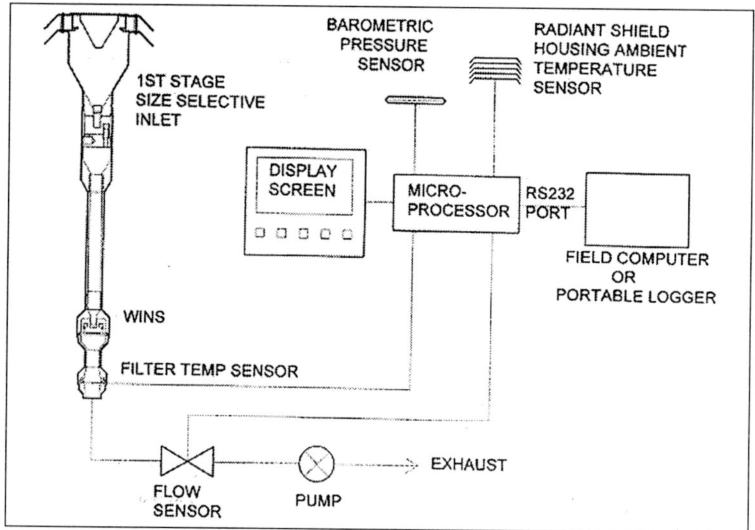

Fig. 6.1: Schematic diagram of a single-channel PM2.5 FRM sampler

FLOW CHART FOR MEASUREMENT OF $PM_{2.5}$
Check the filter for any physical damages
Mark identification number on the filter
Condition the filter in conditioning room/desiccator for 24 hours
Record initial weight
Place the filter on the sampler
Run the sampler for eight hours
Record the flow rate on hourly basis
Remove the filter from the sampler
Keep the exposed filter in a proper container
Record the total time of sampling & average flow rate
Again condition the filter in conditioning room/desiccator for 24 hours
Record final weight
Calculate the concentration of $PM_{2.5}$ in $\mu g/m^3$

GUIDELINES FOR SAMPLING AND ANALYSIS PROTOCOL FOR OZONE IN AMBIENT AIR (CHEMICAL METHOD)

PURPOSE

The purpose of this protocol is to provide guidelines for monitoring of ozone in ambient air.

STANDARD

The national ambient air quality standards for ozone is presented in the table.

Pollutant	Time Weighted Average	Concentration in Ambient Air	
		Industrial, Residential, Rural and other Areas	Ecologically Sensitive Area (Notified by Central Government)
Ozone (O_3), $\mu g/m^3$	8 Hours* 1 Hour**	100 180	100 180

* Annual Arithmetic mean of minimum 104 measurements in a year at a particular site taken twice a week 24 hourly at uniform intervals.

** 24 hourly or 8 hourly or 1 hourly monitored values, as applicable, shall be complied with 98% of the time in a year. 2% of the time, they may exceed the limits but not on two consecutive days of monitoring.

PRINCIPLE OF THE METHOD

Method 411, Air Sampling and Analysis, 3rd Edition (Determination of oxidizing substances in the atmosphere)

Micro-amounts of ozone and the oxidants liberate iodine when absorbed in a 1% solution of potassium iodine buffered at pH 6.8±0.2. The iodine is determined spectro-photometrically by measuring the absorption of tri-iodide ion at 352 nm.

The stoichiometry is approximated by the following reaction:

$$O_3 + 3\,KI + H_2O \rightarrow KI_3 + 2\,KOH + O_2$$

INSTRUMENT/EQUIPMENT

The following items are necessary to perform the monitoring and analysis of ammonia in ambient air:

- Analytical balance
- Vacuum pump: Any suction pump capable of drawing the required sample flow rate of 1 to 2 litre per minute
- Calibrated flow measuring device to control the air flow from 1 to 2 l/min.
- Absorber: All glass midget impinger
- Spectrophotometer: Capable of measuring absorbance at 352 nm.
- Glass wares: low actinic glassware must be used for analysis

REAGENTS/CHEMICALS

All the chemicals should meet specifications of ACS Analytical Reagent grade

- Distilled water
- Absorbing Solution (1% KI in 0.1 m Phosphate Buffer) - Dissolve 13.6 g of potassium dihydrogen phosphate (KH_2PO_4), 14.2 g of disodium hydrogen phosphate (Na_2HPO_4) or 35.8 g of the dodecahydrate salt (Na_2HPO_2. 12 H_2O), and 10.0 g of potassium iodide in sequence and dilute the mixture to 1 L with water. Keep at room temperature for at least 1 day before use. Measure pH and adjust to 6.8 ± 0.2 with NaOH or KH_2PO_4. This solution can be stored for several months in a glass stoppered brown bottle at room temperature without deterioration. It should not be exposed to direct sunlight.
- Stock Solution 0.025 M I_2 (0.05N) - Dissolve 16 g of potassium iodide and 3.173 g of re-sublimed iodine successively and dilute the mixture to exactly 500 ml with water. Keep at room temperature at least 1 day before use. Standardize shortly before use, against 0.025 M $Na_2S_2O_3$. The sodium thiosulfate is standardized against primary standard biiodate [$KH(IO_3)_2$] or potassium dichromate ($K_2Cr_2O_7$).
- *M I_2 Solution* - Pipette exactly 4.00 ml of the 0.025 M Stock solution into a 100 m low actinic volumetric flask and dilute to the mark with absorbing solution. Protect from strong light. Discard after use.

SAMPLING

Place 10 ml of absorbing solution in a standard impinger and sample for one hour at the flow rate of 1 L/min. Do not expose the absorbing reagent to direct sunlight. After sampling measure the volume of sample and transfer to a sample storage bottle.

ANALYSIS

If, appreciable evaporation of the absorbing solution occurs during sampling, add water to bring the liquid volume to 10 ml.

Within 30 to 60 minutes after sample collection, read the absorbance in a cuvette at 352 nm against a reference cuvette containing distilled water. Measure the absorbance of the unexposed reagent and subtract the value from the absorbance of the sample.

CALIBRATION

Preparation of Standards

Calibrating Iodine Solution - For calibration purposes exactly 5.11 ml of the 0.001 M I_2 solution (or equivalent volume for other molarity) is diluted with absorbing solution just before use to 100 ml (final volume) to make the final concentration equivalent to 1 µl of O_3/ml. This solution preparation accounts for the stoichiometry described in Section 3 at standard conditions of 101.3 kPa and 25°C. Discard this solution after use.

Obtain a range of calibration points containing from 1 µl to 10 µl of ozone equivalent per 10.0 ml of solution. Prepare by individually adding 1.0, 2.0, 4.0, 6.0, 8.0 and 10.0 mL of the calibrating iodine solution to 10.0 ml volumetric flasks.

Bring each to the calibration mark with absorbing reagent.

Read the absorbance of each of the prepared calibration solutions at 352 nm against distilled water reference.

Standard Curve

Plot a curve absorbance (Y axis) versus concentration (X axis). Draw a line of best fit and determine the slope. The reciprocal of slope gives the calibration factor (CF).

CALCULATION

$$C\ (O_3\ \mu g/m^3) = (A_s - A_b) \times CF \times 1.962/V_a$$

Where,

$C\ NH_3$ = Concentration of Ammonia in $\mu g/m^3$

A_s = Absorbance of sample

A_b = Absorbance of reagent blank

CF = Calibration factor

V_a = Volume of air sampled in m^3

1.962 = Conversion factor, µl to µg

QUALITY CONTROL

Quality Control (QC) is the techniques that are used to fulfil requirements for quality. The QC procedures for the air sampling and monitoring sections of this protocol include preventative maintenance of equipment, calibration of equipment, analysis of field blanks and lab blanks.

FLOW CHART FOR MEASUREMENT OF OZONE (CHEMICAL METHOD)
Place10 ml of absorbing media in an impinger
Connect it to the gas sampling manifold of gas sampling device (RDS/HVS)
Draw air at a sampling rate of 1 lpm for 60 minutes
Do not expose the absorbing reagent to direct sunlight
Add de ionized water to make up the evaporation loss during sampling and bring the volume to 10 ml.
Prepare calibration graph as recommended in method
Within 30 to 60 minutes after sample collection, read the absorbance in a cuvette at 352 nm against a reference cuvette containing de ionized water
Calculate concentration using calibration graph
Calculate concentration of Ozone in $\mu g/m^3$

GUIDELINES FOR SAMPLING AND ANALYSIS PROTOCOL FOR AMMONIA IN AMBIENT AIR (INDOPHENOL BLUE METHOD)

PURPOSE

The purpose of this protocol is to provide guidelines for monitoring of ammonia in ambient air.

STANDARD

The national ambient air quality standard for ammonia is presented in the table:

Pollutant	Time Weighted Average	Concentration in Ambient Air	
		Industrial, Residential, Rural and other Areas	Ecologically Sensitive Area (Notified by Central Government)
Ammonia (NH_3), µg/m^3	Annual* 24 Hours**	100 400	100 400

* Annual Arithmetic mean of minimum 104 measurements in a year at a particular site taken twice a week 24 hourly at uniform intervals.

** 24 hourly or 8 hourly or 1 hourly monitored values, as applicable, shall be complied with 98% of the time in a year. 2% of the time, they may exceed the limits but not on two consecutive days of monitoring.

PRINCIPLE OF THE METHOD

Indophenol method (Method 401, Air Sampling and Analysis, 3rd Edition) Ammonia in the atmosphere is collected by bubbling a measured volume of air through a dilute solution of sulphuric acid to form ammonium sulphate. The ammonium sulphate formed in the sample is analyzed colorimetrically by reaction with phenol and alkaline sodium hypochlorite to produce indophenol. The reaction is accelerated by the addition of Sodium Nitroprusside as catalyst.

INSTRUMENT/EQUIPMENT

The following items are necessary to perform the monitoring and analysis of ammonia in ambient air:

- Analytical balance
- Vacuum pump to maintain a flow rate up to 5 litre per minute
- Calibrated flow measuring device to control the air flow from 1 to 2 litre/min.
- Absorber: a midget impinger or a fritted bubbler
- Spectrophotometer capable of measuring absorbance at 630 nm.
- Glass ware: low actinic glass wares must be used for analysis

REAGENTS/CHEMICALS

All the chemicals should meet specifications of ACS Analytical Reagent grade

- Distilled water
- N Sulphuric Acid (Absorbing solution)
- Sodium Nitroprusside
- 6.75 M sodium hydroxide
- Sodium hypochlorite solution
- Phenol solution 45% v/v
- Sodium phosphate
- Ammonium chloride or Ammonium Sulfate
- Hydrochloric acid
- Ammonia stock solution (1 mg NH_3/ml)
- Ammonia working solution (10 µg NH_3/ml) (Prepare fresh daily)

SAMPLING

Place 10 ml of absorbing solution in an impinger and sample for one hour at the flow rate of 1 to 2 L/min. After sampling measure the volume of sample and transfer to a sample storage bottle.

ANALYSIS

Transfer contents of the sample bottle to a 25 ml glass stopper graduated cylinder. Maintain all the solutions and sample at 25 C. Add 2 ml buffer. Add 5 ml of working phenol solution, mix, and fill to about 22 ml. Add 2.5 ml of working hypochlorite solution and rapidly mix. Dilute to 25 ml, mix and store in the dark for 30 minutes to develop colour. Measure the absorbance of the solution at 630 nm on a spectrophotometer using 1 cm cells. Prepare a reagent blank and field blank and measure the absorbance as done in the analysis of samples.

CALIBRATION

Preparation of Standards

Pipet 0.5, 1.0, 1.5, 2.0 ml of working standard solution in to 25 ml glass stoppered graduated cylinders. Fill to 10 ml mark with absorbing solution. A reagent blank with 10 ml absorbing solution is also prepared. Add reagents to each cylinder as in the procedure for analysis. Read the absorbance of each standard against reagent blank.

Standard Curve

Plot a curve absorbance (Y axis) versus concentration (X axis). Draw a line of best fit and determine the slope. The reciprocal of slope gives the calibration factor (CF).

CALCULATION

$$C\ (NH_3\ \mu g/m^3) = (A_s - A_b) \times CF/V_a$$

Where,

$C\ NH_3$ = Concentration of Ammonia in $\mu g/m^3$

A_s = Absorbance of sample

A_b = Absorbance of reagent blank

CF = Calibration factor

V_a = Volume of air sampled in m^3

QUALITY CONTROL

Quality Control (QC) is the techniques that are used to fulfill requirements for quality. The QC procedures for the air sampling and monitoring sections of this protocol include preventative maintenance of equipment, calibration of equipment, analysis of field blanks and lab blanks.

FLOW CHART FOR MEASUREMENT OF AMMONIA
Dilute 10ml of concentrated HCl (12M) to 100 ml with distilled water Wash the glassware with the water and finally rinse it thrice with distilled water
Adjust the Flow rate at 1L/min of the rotameter and the manifolds of the attached APM 411/APM 460Dx
Place 10 ml of absorbing media in each midget impinger for samples and field blanks Assemble (in order) prefilter and holder, flowmeter, impinger and pump Sample at the rate of 1L/min for 1hour duration
Record the sampling time, average flow rate and final volume of the solution After the sample collection, transfer the solution in the impinger to polyethylene bottle and recap it tightly for transport to laboratory for analysis
Prepare the absorbing media, various reagents and working solutions as per the method described in protocol Standardize the sodium thiosulphate solution by titrating it against potassium iodate and Sodium hypochlorite by titrating it against standardized sodium thiosulphate solution
Take 25 ml measuring flasks and rinse with distilled water. Transfer the contents from polyethylene bottles to 25 ml measuring flasks (Maintain all the solutions at 25°C) Add 2 ml of buffer (to maintain pH) Add 5 ml of working phenol solution, mix, fill to about 22 ml with distilled water and then add 2.5 ml of working hypochlorite solution & mix rapidly Store in the dark for 30 mins to develop colour. Measure the absorbance of the solution at 630 nm using UV Spectrophotometer
Pipette 0.5, 1.0 and 1.5 ml of working standard solution (working ammonia solution) in 25 ml measuring flasks Fill to 10 ml mark with absorbing solution (0.1 M H_2SO_4). Add the reagents as to each flask as in the procedure for analysis Read the absorbance of each standard against the reagent blank
Plot the calibration curve
Calculate the concentration of NH_3 in $\mu g/m^3$

GUIDELINES FOR SAMPLING AND ANALYSIS OF BENZO(A)PYRENE & OTHER PAHS IN AMBIENT AIR (SOLVENT EXTRACTION & GC ANALYSIS)

PURPOSE

The purpose of this protocol is to provide guidelines for monitoring of Benzo (a) Pyrene (BaP) in ambient air.

Benzo (a) Pyrene (BaP) is one of the most important constituent of PAH compounds and also one of the most potent carcinogens. This can be measured in both particulate phase and vapour phase. In the vapour phase the concentration of B(a)P is significantly less than the particulate phase. Therefore, more care to be taken for the measurement of Benzo (a) Pyrene in the particulate phase. The molecular formula of B(a)P is $C_{20}H_{12}$ having molecular weight 252 and structural formula is given in following figure:

Structural Formula of Benzo (a) Pyrene (BaP)

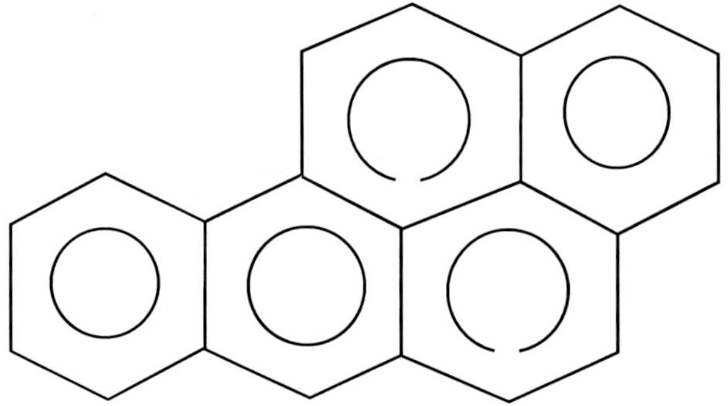

STANDARD

The national ambient air quality standard for Benzo(a)pyrene is presented in table:

Pollutant	Time weighted Average	Concentration in Ambient Air (ng/m^3)	
		Industrial, Residential, Rural and other Areas	Ecologically Sensitive Area (Notified by Central Government)
Benzo(a)pyrene	Annual	01	01

* Annual Arithmetic mean of minimum 104 measurements in a year at a particular site taken twice a week 24 hourly at uniform intervals.

** 24 hourly or 8 hourly or 1 hourly monitored values, as applicable, shall be complied with 98% of the time in a year. 2% of the time, they may exceed the limits but not on two consecutive days of monitoring.

PRINCIPLE OF THE METHOD

It is based on BIS method IS 5182 (Part 12): 2004 and USEPA method (TO-13). This method is designed to collect particulate phase PAHs in ambient air and fugitive emissions and to determine individual PAH compounds using capillary gas chromatograph equipped with flame ionization detector. It is a high volume ($1.2m^3/min$) sampling method capable of detecting sub.ng/m^3 concentration of PAH in 24 hours sample (i.e. collected in 3 shifts of 8 hour each with 480 m^3 sampling volume of air).

EQUIPMENT/INSTRUMENTS

PM_{10} high volume sampler, Whatman Glass fibre (EPM-2000) or Equivalent Filter Paper, Ultra Sonicator (~40kHz frequency), Rotary Evaporator (Buchi type), Gas Chromatograph with Flame Ionization Detector fitted with Capillary Column (H.P./Agilent Ultra 2 or equivalent, length 25 meter × 0.320mm, 0.17µm or more), Syringes (5 & 10 micro litre capacity), Variable volume micropipettes (0.5 & 1.0 ml capacity), Beakers (250 ml), Amber colour Vials 3ml and 5ml capacity, Chromatographic column (200-250 mm*10mmwith Teflon stopcock).

CHEMICAL/SOLVENTS

All chemicals, calibration/reference standards of B(a)P, other PAHs, Triphenyl benzene (internal standard, ultra residue grade) solvents like Toluene, Cyclohexane (with minimum residue less than 0.005%) etc.) & other chemicals like Silica -Gel (6080 mesh size) should be of highest purity & of reputed make with traceability/purity and analysis certificate.

SAMPLING

Instrument/Filter Selection

24 hr. sampling using PM_{10} high volume sampler with 8 hourly samples using EPM2000 glass fibre or equivalent filter.

Sampling Frequency

Sampling is done twice a week, total of 104 days monitoring in a year. Particulate laden Benzo(a)Pyrene samples are collected on glass fibre filter (EPM 2000 or equivalent) using PM_{10} sampler at a flow rate of more than $1m^3$/min per minute, at selected location(s).

Sampling Height

Sampling height may be between 3-10 meters from the ground level for ambient air quality monitoring.

Sample Filter Storage

After sampling, filters are kept in the controlled laboratory conditions (20-25°C) in an envelope marked with necessary identification information if processed immediately, otherwise wrap the filters in Aluminium foil & kept it in refrigerator at 4°C in dark to avoid photo oxidation of PAHs.

Sample Processing

(a) Extraction

Filter papers (half of all the filters papers collected in a day) are cut into strips using scissors and transfer to 250 ml beaker. Add ~50 ml. of Toluene (GC/HPLC grade). These samples are extracted with toluene using ultra sonic bath for about 30 minutes. Repeat the procedure twice (50ml × 2 times) for complete extraction. Alternatively, sample can be extracted using soxhlet extraction apparatus for about 8 hr. with Toluene and repeat it twice. Sample processing steps are shown in figure 6.2.

(b) Filtration

Filter the extracted samples with Whatman filter paper no. 41 containing 2 gm of Anhydrous Sodium Sulphate (to remove moisture).

(c) Concentration

After filtration, the filtrate is concentrated using Rotary vacuum evaporator (Figure 6.3) to 2ml final volume.

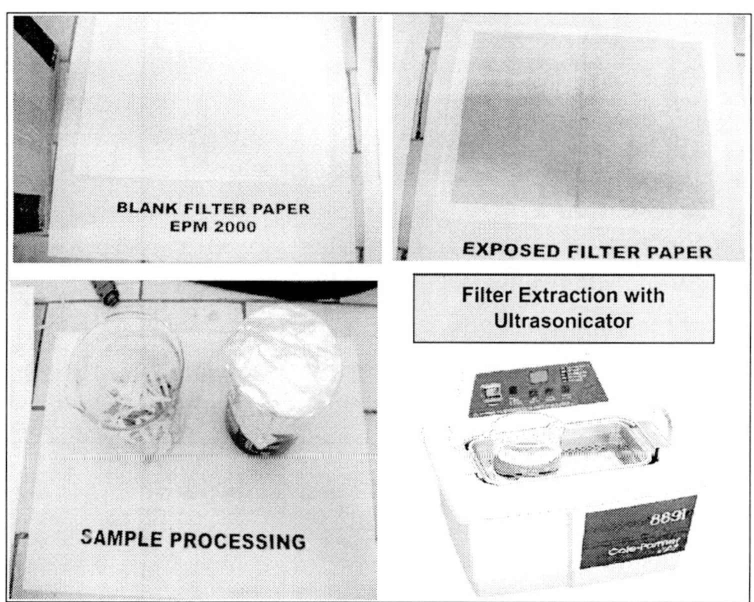

Fig. 6.2: Sample Processing

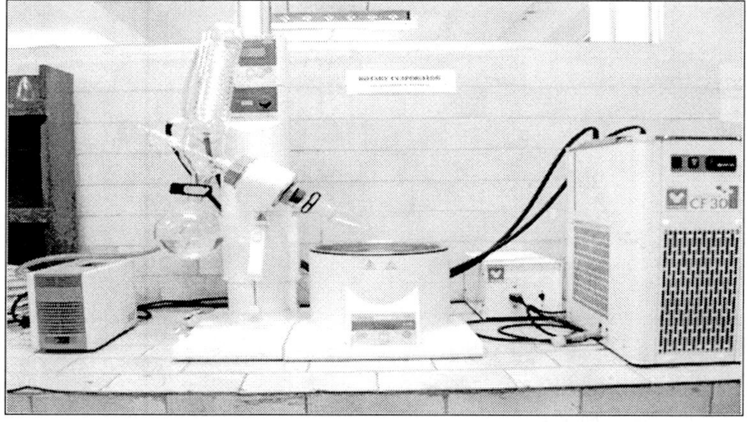

Fig. 6.3: Rotary Evaporator for Sample Concentration

(d) Clean-up with silica Gel

To clean up the impurities, pass 2 ml of concentrated sample through silica gel column (pre conditioned, 60-80 mesh, and 200-250mm×10 mm with Teflon stopcock). After cleaning add 5ml cyclohexane and collect the elute in 25 ml beaker. Repeat the process for at least 3 times and collect it in the same beaker. Alternatively Solid Phase Extraction (SPE) may be used for clean up the impurities of sample.

(e) Re-concentration with rotary vacuum evaporator

The Cleaned up extract/filtrate (approximately 17 ml) is further concentrated using rotary evaporator and it is evaporated to nearly dryness with Nitrogen.

(f) Final Sample volume

The dried sample is re-dissolved in 1ml of toluene and transfer into 4 or 5 ml amber vials final analysis.

(g) Extracted Sample Storage

Cover/Cap the sample vials/tubes and mark with necessary identification.

Keep it in refrigerator at 4°C prior to the analysis as in figure 6.4.

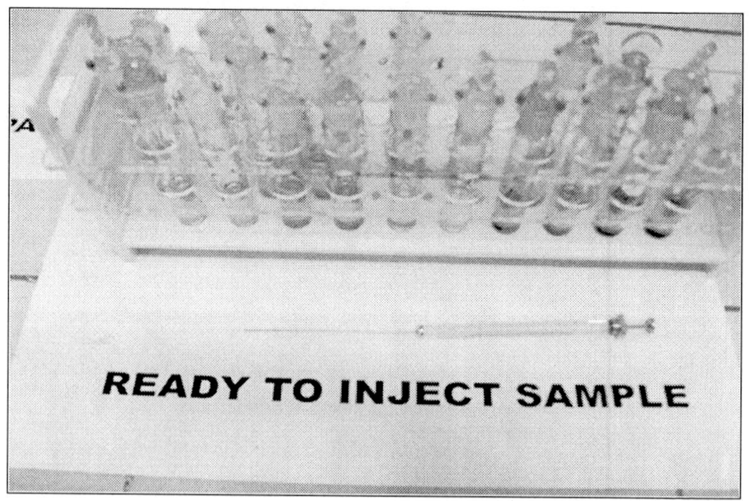

Fig. 6.4: Ready to Inject B(a)P Samples

ANALYSIS/INSTRUMENT SET-UP

GC Conditions: Injector: 300°C

FID Temp: 320°C

Column: Ultra -2 (25m Length, 320μm diameter, 0.17μ) or equivalent.

Oven: 120°C →2 min hold → 7°C/min → 300°C → 10 min hold

Run Time: 37.71 minutes Carrier gas flow (N_2): 0.50 ml/min Gases for FID Flame:

H_2 flow: 40 ml/min

Zero grade air flow: 400 ml/min

Preparation of Standard Calibration Mixture

Stock Standard Solution PAH mix standard solution of 16 Compounds including B(a)P (Dr. Ehrenstorfer, Germany make PAH mix 63) of concentration 1000mg/l (or 1000ng/μl) in Toluene.

Working Standard Solution Working Standard Solutions (5, 10, 15, 20, 25 ng/μl concentrations) are prepared from stock solution by diluting 200 to 40 times the stock B(a)P or other PAH solution of 1000mg/l (or 1000ng/μl) concentration with Toluene.

Internal Standard 1, 2, 3-Tri Phenyl Benzene of concentration ~1000ng/μl is added in the working standard solution so that the final concentration of Internal standard is 10 ng/μl.

Calibration of GC

Internal Calibration

Inject 1μl of each Working Standard (5, 10, 15, 20, 25 ng/μl) in triplicate and plot the area ratio of analyte PAH Compound [i.e. B(a)P] and the corresponding internal standard against the concentration for each compound and internal standard. The instrument is calibrated as per its manual/software.

External Calibration

Inject 1µl of each Working Standard (5, 10, 15, 20, 25 ng/µl) made in Toluene into GC-FID and plot the area of analyte viz. PAH Compound [i.e.B(a)P] against the corresponding concentration of the standard. The instrument is calibrated as per its manual/software.

The quantification of that analyte will be based on peak area response of respective compounds with respect to working calibration standard, that is calibration factor (the ratio of response to the amount of mass injected).The retention time of various PAHs compounds are obtained under the above GC conditions.

Sample injection

Take 2µl of sample from the amber vial using standard gas tight syringe and inject in the Capillary GC-FID instrument for analysis. Record the resulting concentration of each PAH compound including B(a)P. A 10ng/µl concentration B(a)P or other PAH standards are to be injected in GC/FID instrument with every batch of samples. As a control Internal Standard of 10 ng/µl conc. is added to each sample prior to the analysis in case of internal calibration is used.

CALCULATIONS

Calculate the concentration in ng/µl of each identified analyte or B(a)P in the sample extract (Cs) as follows:

Calculate the air volume from the periodic flow reading taken during sampling using the following equation:

$$V = Q \times T$$

Where,

Q = Average flow rate of sampling m^3/min T = sampling time, in min.

V = total sample volume at ambient conditions in m^3

Concentration of analyte i.e B(a)P:

The concentration of PAH compound or Benzo(a)pyrene in ng/m^3 in the air sampled is given by:

$$C\ (ng\ /m^3) = Cs * Ve/Vi * Vs$$

Where,

Cs: Concentration of Benzo (a) pyrene in ng / µl in the sample extract recorded by GC.

Ve: Final volume of extract in µl (i.e 1000)

Vi: Injection Volume (i.e 1µl)

Vs: Volume of air sample in m^3

QUALITY CONTROL

For recovery efficiency isotopically labelled B(a)P or other PAH surrogate standards are added to the samples prior to extraction & analysis. The recoveries should fall between 75 125 % preferably.

A 10 ng/µl concentration B(a)P or other PAH standards are to be injected in GC/FID instrument with every batch of samples or daily as a control. If substantial variation is found in observed concentration, instrument should be recalibrated.

Internal Standard of 10 ng/µl conc. is added to each sample prior to the analysis in case of internal calibration is used.

DETECTION LIMIT

The minimum detectable concentration in terms of B(a)P for a sampling period of 8 hour (with about 480 m^3 of air passed) will be 1ng/m^3 assuming 1.0 ml as the final volume of sample extract after clean-up and detectable concentration of 1ng/µl of that sample extract. High resolution capillary mass spectrometry or high pressure liquid chromatography can improve sensitivity down to 1ng/m^3.

FLOW CHART FOR MEASUREMENT OF BENZO(A)PYRENE
EPM 2000 filter paper
Ultrasonic extraction with Toluene (50 ml · 3 times)
Filter & dry with Anhydrous Sodium Sulphate
Concentration with Rotary Evaporator
Clean up with Silica Gel Column Chromatography
Elution with Cyclo-Hexane (5 ml · 3 times)

(Contd...)

Evaporate to nearly dryness under Nitrogen	
Re-dissolved in 0.5 to 1.0 ml Toluene	Re-dissolved in 2.5 ml Methanol
Capillary GC-FID or GC-MS	HPLC/UV-Fluorescence Detector

GUIDELINES FOR SAMPLING AND ANALYSIS OF LEAD, NICKEL AND ARSENIC IN AMBIENT AIR (ATOMIC ABSORPTION SPECTROPHOTOMETER METHOD)

PURPOSE

The purpose of this protocol is to provide guidelines for monitoring of lead, nickel and arsenic in ambient air.

STANDARD

The national ambient air quality standards for lead, nickel and arsenic is presented in the table. (*See on next page*)

PRINCIPLE OF THE METHOD

The Atomic Absorption Spectroscopy (AAS) technique makes use of absorption spectrometry to assess the concentration of an analyte in the sample. The method is based on active sampling using PM_{10} High Volume Sampler and then sample analysis is done by atomic absorption spectrophoto-meter.

Pollutant	Time Weighted Average	Concentration in Ambient Air	
		Industrial, Residential, Rural and other Areas	Ecologically Sensitive Area (Notified by Central Government)
Lead (Pb), $\mu g/m^3$	Annual* 24 Hours**	0.50 1.0	0.50 1.0
Nickel (Ni), ng/m^3	Annual *	20	20
Arsenic(As), ng/m^3	Annual*	06	06

* Annual Arithmetic mean of minimum 104 measurements in a year at a particular site taken twice a week 24 hourly at uniform intervals.

** 24 hourly or 8 hourly or 1 hourly monitored values, as applicable, shall be complied with 98% of the time in a year. 2% of the time, they may exceed the limits but not on two consecutive days of monitoring.

INSTRUMENT/EQUIPMENT

The following items are necessary to perform the protocol for monitoring of lead and nickel in ambient air:

- PM_{10} sampler (high volume design based)
- Hot plate
- Microwave Digestive System
- Analytical balance
- Digestion chamber
- Polyethylene or polypropylene bottle
- Glasswares
- Top loading orifice kit
- FAAS (Flame Atomic Absorption Spectrophotometer) or
- GFAAS (Graphite Furnace Atomic Absorption Spectrophotometer)

REAGENTS/CHEMICALS

- Filter Paper: EPM 2000 or equivalent, 20.3 × 25.4 cm (8 × 10 in)
- Hydrochloric Acid (HCl) Concentrated (AR grade)
- Nitric Acid (HNO_3) Concentrated (AR grade)
- Sulphuric Acid (H_2SO_4) Concentrated (AR grade)
- Metal Standard Solutions (Certified standard)
- Sodium borohydride (GR/AR grade).
- Potassium iodide (GR/AR grade)
- Distilled/De-ionized

SAMPLING

Sampling procedure

Tilt back the inlet and secure it according to manufacturer's instructions. Loosen the face-plate wing-nuts and remove the face plate. Remove the filter from its jacket and centre it on the support screen with the rough side of the filter facing upwards. Replace the face-plate and tighten the wing-nuts to secure the rubber gasket against the filter edge. Gently lower the inlet. For automatically flow-controlled units, record the designated flow rate on the data sheet. Record the reading of the elapsed time meter. The specified length of sampling is commonly 8 hours or 24 hours. During this period, several reading (hourly) of flow rate should be taken. After the required time of sampling, record the flow meter reading and take out the filter media from the sampler and put in a container or envelope.

Sample storage

After collecting samples, transport the filters to the laboratory, taking care to minimize contamination and loss of the sample. Glass fibre filters should be transported or shipped in a shipping envelope. Store these protective envelopes up to 30 C until analysis. The maximum sample holding times is usually 180 days. Analyze the samples within 180 days.

ANALYSIS

Extraction of Samples

The collected sample on glass fibre filters may be extracted by either hot plate procedure or by microwave extraction (Method IO-3.1).

Microwave extraction

Cut 1"×8" strip or half the filter from the 8"×10" filter sample and place on its edge in a labelled centrifuge tube using vinyl gloves or plastic forceps. Using the plastic forceps, crush the filter strip down into the lower portion of the centrifuge tube to ensure acid volume will cover entire filter. Add 10.0 ml of the extraction solution to each of the centrifuge tubes (3% conc. HNO_3 and 8% conc. HCl). Place the centrifuge tubes in a Teflon vessel containing 31 ml of deionized water. Place the vessel caps with the pressure release valves on the vessels hand-tight and tighten using the capping station to a constant torque of 12 ft-lb. Place the vessels in the microwave carousel. Connect each sample vessel to the overflow vessel using the Teflon connecting tubes. Place the carousel containing the 12 vessels on to the turntable of the microwave unit. Irradiate the sample vessels at 486 W (power output) for 23 min.

Allow the pressure to dissipate, then remove the carousel containing the vessels and cool in tap water for 10 min. using the caping station uncap the microwave vessels, remove the labelled centrifuge tube containing samples. Add 10ml of deionized water to each centrifuge tube. Cap the centrifuge tube tightly and mix the contents thoroughly for 2-3 minutes to complete extraction. The final extraction volume is 20ml based upon the above procedure. Filter the extracted fluid with Whatman No. 41 and make up the final volume to 100 ml, the filtered sample is now ready for analysis.

Hot plate procedure

Cut a 1" × 8" strip or half the filter from the 8" × 10" filter using a stainless steel pizza cutter. Place the filter in a beaker using vinyl gloves or plastic forceps. Cover the filter with the extraction solution (3% HNO_3 & 8% HCl). Place beaker on the hotplate, contained in a fume hood, and reflux gently while covered with a watch glass for 30 min. Do not allow sample to dry. Remove the beakers from the hot-plate and allow to cool. Rinse the beaker walls and wash with distilled water. Add approximately 10 mL reagent water to the remaining filter material in the beaker and allow to stand for at least 30 min. Transfer the extraction fluid in the beaker to a 100 mL volumetric flask or other graduated vessel. Rinse the beaker and any remaining solid material with distilled water and add the rinses to the flask. Dilute to the mark with distilled water (Type I) water and shake. The final extraction solution concentration is 3% HNO_3/8% HCl. The filtered sample is now ready for analysis

Analysis of samples

Instrument/Equipment

A light beam containing the corresponding wavelength of the energy required to raise the atoms of the analyte from the ground state to the excited state is directed through the flame or furnace. This wavelength is observed by a monochromator and a detector that measure the amount of light absorbed by the element, hence the number of atoms in the ground state in the flame or furnace. A hollow cathode lamp for the element being determined provides a source of that metal's particular absorption wavelength.

The method describes both flame atomic absorption (FAA) spectroscopy and graphite furnace atomic absorption (GFAA) spectroscopy. Atomic Absorption Spectrophotometer - analyze the metals by Flame, if results are below detection limit then go for GTA. Arsenic is analyzed by Flame – VGA.

Flame Procedure

Set the atomic absorption spectrophotometer for the standard condition as follows: choose the correct hollow cathode lamp, align the instrument, position the monochromator at the value recommended by the manufacturer, select the proper monochromator slit width, set the light source current, ignite the flame, regulate the flow of fuel and oxidant, adjust the burner for maximum absorption and stability and balance the meter. Run a series of standards of the metal of interest and construct a calibration curve. Aspirate the blanks and samples. Dilute samples that exceed the calibration range. For Lead (Pb) and Nickel (Ni), the wavelength required for analysis is 217nm and 232nm respectively. Where as in case of Arsenic (As), the VGA should attach with Flame and the wavelength required for analysis is 193.7nm.

Furnace Procedure

As a general rule, samples that can be analyzed by flame or furnace may be more conveniently run with flame since flame atomic absorption is faster, simpler and has fewer interference problems. Tube life depends on sample matrix and atomization temperature. A conservative estimate of tube life is about 50 firings. Read the metal value in ìg/L from the calibration curve or directly from the read-out of the instrument.

CALIBRATION

Prepare standard solutions from the stock solutions. Select at least three standards to cover linear range as recommended by method. Aspirate the standards into the flame or inject the standards into the furnace and record the absorbance. Prepare the calibration graph by plotting absorbance and concentration in µg/ml.

Preparation of Standards

For each metal that is to be determined, standards of known concentration must be acquired commercially certified standards.

Standard Curve

Standard curve is prepared by using standard solutions of known concentration.

QUALITY CONTROL

To produce good quality data, perform quality control checks and independent audits of the measurement process; document their data and use materials, instruments and measurement procedures that can be traced to an appropriate standard of reference. Shewart's analytical quality control chart should be maintained for good quality data. Detection limit and working range for each metal should be followed of the working instrument.

Precision

Analyze the pretreated sub-samples. Calculate the standard deviation (S) and coefficient of variation (CV) where CV = S.100/mean value. If the CV is greater than 10%, check the whole procedure for possible errors and/or contamination. The precision of the method is normally better than ± 5% at the 95% confidence level.

Accuracy

Analyze the pretreated Certified Reference Material (CRM) or internal reference material. Calculate the mean and the standard deviation. If the value given for the CRM is within the interval of mean ± standard deviation, the method has the required accuracy. If not, check the whole procedure.

CALCULATIONS

Sample Air Volume

Sample air volume can be calculated by using the following equation:

$$V = (Q)\ (t)$$

Where,

V = volume of air, m^3

Q = average sampling rate, m^3/min.

t = time in minutes.

Metal Concentration

$$C = (Ms - Mb) \times Vs \times Fa/V \times Ft$$

Where,

C = concentration, µg metal/m^3.

Ms = metal concentration µg/mL

Mb = blank concentration µg/mL

Vs = total volume of extraction in mL

Fa = total area of exposed filter in cm^2

V = Volume of air sampled in m^3

Ft = Area of filter taken for digestion in cm^2

FLOW CHART FOR SAMPLE PROCESSING OF LEAD, NICKEL AND ARSENIC IN AMBIENT AIR
Collect the particulate matter on glass fibre filter (EPM 2000 or equivalent) using PM_{10} sampler (High Volume Sampling)
Divide the filter paper in two equal parts
Half portion of filter paper for the measurement of lead, nickel and arsenic
Extract the sample by either hot plate procedure or by microwave extraction
Analysis of extracted sample using recommended method

FLOW CHART FOR MEASUREMENT OF LEAD AND NICKEL BY FLAMEATOMIC ABSORPTION SPECTROPHOTOMETER: METHOD I (METHOD IO-3 ,IO-3.2)
Switch on Atomic Absorption Spectrophotometer
Select and set the Hollow Cathode Lamp of desired metal and programming the instrument accordingly
Adjust and align the instrument as per requirement
Switch on Compressor for Air and Open the required gas cylinders (Air - Acetylene for Flame analysis), Ignite the Flame
Calibration with metal standards as recommended in method
Prepare calibration graph
Analyze the digested samples
Calculate the concentration using calibration graph

FLOW CHART FOR MEASUREMENT OF LEAD, NICKEL AND ARSENIC BY GRAPHITE TUBE-ATOMIC ABSORPTION SPECTROPHOTOMETER: METHOD II (METHOD IO-3,IO-3.2)
Switch on Atomic Absorption Spectrophotometer
Place the furnace, adjust and align the instrument as per requirement of GTA
Select and set the Hollow Cathode Lamp of desired metal and programming the instrument accordingly for standards and samples
Switch on Chiller and keep the Temperature at 20° C Open the Nitrogen gas
Clean the Graphite Tube with a firing
Click the START Button
Calibration with metal standards as recommended in method
Prepare calibration graph
Analyze the digested samples
Calculate the concentration using calibration graph
Note: Always follow the instructions of the Instrument/Operational manual given by the supplier

FLOW CHART FOR MEASUREMENT OF ARSENIC BY FLAME- ATOMIC ABSORPTION SPECTROPHOTOMETER USING VAPOUR GENERATION ASSEMBLY (VGA): METHOD III (Standard Method- American Public Health Association (APHA), 20th Edition, 1998)
Switch on Atomic Absorption Spectrophotometer
Select and set the Hollow Cathode Lamp of Arsenic and programming the instrument accordingly
Adjust and align the instrument as per requirement –VGA
Switch on Compressor for Air and Open the required gas cylinders (Air - Acetylene for Flame analysis and Nitrogen for Hydride Generator)
Ignite the Flame
Check the flow rate of Hydride Generator
Calibration with Arsenic standards as recommended in method
Prepare calibration graph
Analyze the digested samples
Calculate the concentration using calibration graph
Note: Always follow the instructions of the Instrument/Operational manual given by the supplier

FIELD DATA SHEET FOR GASEOUS POLLUTANTS

Station:	Date:				Graph Factor		SO_2		Graph Factor		NO_2	
Shift	Ist Shift				IInd Shift				IIIrd Shift			
Monitoring Period	06:00AM-10:00AM		10:00AM-02:00 PM		02:00PM-06:00PM		06:00PM-10:00PM		10:00PM-02:00AM		02:00AM-06:00AM	
Parameter	SO_2	NO_2	SO_2	NO_2	SO_2	NO_2	SO_2	NO_2	SO_2	NO_2	SO_2	NO_2
Hourly Flow Rate (lpm)												
Average Flow Rate (lpm)												
Total Operation Time (Minutes)												
Initial Volume of Sample (ml)												
Final Volume of Sample (ml)												
Volume Taken For Analysis (ml)												
Total Volume of Air Sampled (lit.)												
Absorbance (Blank)												
Absorbance (Sample)												
Concentration (μg/m³)												
24 Hourly Average SO_2 (μg/m³):					**24 Hourly Average NO_2 (μg/m³):**							
Remarks:												
Name & Signature of Official on duty												
Analyzed by:												

RESULTS DATA SHEET FOR GASEOUS POLLUTANTS

Location:										Month:							Year:			
TIME (Hrs.)	06-10		10-14		14-18		18-22		22-02		02-06		4 HRS. MAX		24 HRS. AVG		8 HRS. AVG PM_{10}			24 HRS. AVG
PARAMETER/ DATE	SO_2	NO_2	SO_2	NO_2	SO_2	NO_2	SO_2	NO_2	SO_2	NO_2	SO_2	NO_2	SO_2	NO_2	SO_2	NO_2	06-14	14-22	22-06	PM_{10}

Note: All values are expressed in $\mu g/m^3$

Weather Condition: Clear/Cloudy/Rainy

Name & Signature of Official on Duty: **Checked by:**

DATA SHEET FOR PARTICULATE MATTER (Size less than 10 μm) or PM_{10}

Station:		Date:	
Shift			
Monitoring Duration			
Filter Paper No.			
Hourly Flow Rate (m^3/minute)			
Average Flow Rate (m^3/minute)			
Total Operation Time (Minutes)			
Initial Weight of Filter Paper (gms.)			
Final Weight of Filter Paper (gms.)			
Dust Contents (gms.)			
Total Volume of Air Sampled (m^3)			
Concentration (μg/m^3)			
24 Hourly Average SPM (μg/m^3):			
Remarks:			
Name & Signature of Official on Duty:			
Analyzed by:			

SAMPLE TRACKING SHEET ($PM_{2.5}$)

Filter Paper Nos.					Sender's or Operator's Signature	Received by (Signature)
F.Paper Type						
Lot/Batch No.						
Site Description						
Date of Sampling						
Inspection	Date of inspection	Inspection done by		Certified by		
Lab Code						
Pre-conditioning	Nature	Date and Time	Done by	Certified by		
Pre-weighing	Date and Time	Weighed by	Balance Calibration (Y/N)	Control weight Status		
Dispatch detail	Date	To (Specify Sites)				
Filter Receiving	Date & Time	Sites	Sampling date & time	Condition of filters		
Post Conditioning	Nature	Date and Time	Done by	Certified by		
Post-weighing	Date & Time	Weighed by	Balance Calibration (Y/N)	Control weight Status		
Dispatch Detail	Date & time	To (Specify Lab)	Parameters	Results Expected by the date		

$PM_{2.5}$ ANALYSIS REPORT

Name of the Project of Executing Agency : Name

Sampling Location ID and Name :

Monitoring Season :

Date and Time of Monitoring of Instrument used : ID

Last date of Calibration :

Field Sampling Done By :

Analysis Done By :

Filter ID :

Start time	Closing time	Initial Weight (mg)	Final weight (mg)	Flow rate (LPM)	Air Volume (m^3)

Calculation

Volume of air passed (V) = Sampling Duration (Min) X LPM (Average)

Dust collected on Filter (M) = (Final weight – Initial weight) * 1000 µg

Concentration = M / V µg/m^3

Remarks

Meteorological conditions: Temperature – (Min & Max)

% RH – (Min & Max)

Rain fall –

Sampling Stoppage time (if any) with reason:

Name & Signature of Field Operator

Name & Signature of Analyst

Report Checked by (Supervisor)

Report Approved by (Officer in charge)

DATA SHEET FOR OZONE IN AMBIENT AIR

Monitoring Duration	Average Flow Rate (lpm)	Total Sampling Time (Minutes)	Total Volume of Air Sampled (lit.)	Volume of Sample (ml)	Absorbance (Blank)	Absorbance (Sample)	Conc. (μg/m³)
0600-0700							
0700-0800							
0800-0900							
0900-1000							
1000-1100							
1100-1200							
1200-1300							
1300-1400							
1400-1500							
1500-1600							
1600-1700							
1700-1800							
1800-1900							
1900-2000							
2000-2100							
2100-2200							
2200-2300							
2300-2400							
2400-0100							
0100-0200							
0200-0300							
0300-0400							
0400-0500							
0500-0600							

Data Sheet for Ozone

Month: Station:

Duration Datefl	06-07	07-08	08-09	09-10	10-11	11-12	12-13	13-14	14-15	15-16	16-17	17-18	18-19	19-20	20-21	21-22	22-23	23-24	24-01	01-02	02-03	03-04	04-05	05-06	

Concentrations in $\mu g/m^3$

FIELD DATA SHEET (BaP/PAH MONITORING)

Monitoring Location Details: Sheet No.———

Date & time of start	Date & time of close	Run Time in Minutes
Instrument Make & S.No.	Average Flow Rate	Total Air Volume
Filter Paper No	Final Weight (gm)	Initial Weight (gm)
Net Weight (gm)	PM_{10} Conc. (ug/m^3)	Special Weather Note (Rainy/cloudy/Sunny/ Windy/stormy Day)
Pl fill which ever Shift applicable		

Monitoring team members (Names with Signatures & Dates):

Time	Mano-meter Reading m^3/min	Re Ti adi mengr	Time	Mano-meter Reading m^3/min	Re Ti adi mengr	Time	Mano-meter Reading m^3/min	Re Ti Adimengr
6.00			14.00			22.00		
7.00			15.00			23.00		
8.00			16.00			24.00		
9.00			17.00			01.00		
10.00			18.00			02.00		
11.00			19.00			03.00		
12.00			20.00			04.00		
13.00			21.00			05.00		
14.00			22.00			06.00		
Avg. Flow m^3/min			Avg. Flow m^3/min			Avg. Flow m^3/min		

1____________ 2.____________ 3.____________

Project Coordinator (Name with Signature): ____________

AIR LAB DIVISION
BaP/PAH ANALYSIS REPORT

Report S. No.________________ Date:________________

S.No.	Sampling Location	Sample Details	Date of Sampling	Time of Sampling	Benzo(a) Pyrene (ng/m^3)	TPAH (ng/m^3) (if analysed)
1.						
2.						
3.						
4.						
5.						
6.						

Note: Sample analyzed using Capillary GC-FID.

(Analyst) (Supervisor) (I/C –Laboratory)

DATA SHEET FOR PARTICULATE MATTER
(Size less than 10 µm) or PM_{10}

Station:		Date:	
Shift			
Monitoring Duration			
Filter Paper No.			
Hourly Flow Rate (m^3/minute)			
Average Flow Rate (m^3/minute)			
Total Operation Time (Minutes)			
Initial Weight of Filter Paper (gms.)			
Final Weight of Filter Paper (gms.)			
Dust Contents (gms.)			
Total Volume of Air Sampled (m^3)			
Concentration (µg/m^3)			
24 Hourly Average SPM (µg/m^3):			
Remarks:			
Name & Signature of Official on Duty:			
Analysed by:			

Trace Metals Analysis Report

1. Report no. & issue date :
2. Name of the Project :
3. Sample matrix :
4. Date & time of sample collection :
5. Samples collected by :
6. Date & time of sample receipt :
7. Date of sample analysis :
8. Sample registration no. & date :
9. Sampling plan reference :
10. Test method reference :
11. Report sent to (Name & Address) :

S. No.	Sample Code	Pb (µg/ml)	Ni (µg/ml)	As (µg/ml)

Statement:

1. The results relate only to the samples tested.
2. The report shall not be reproduced except in full, without the written approval of the laboratory.

Analyst **Supervisor** **In-Charge**

Analysis report of Metals

Month: Station:

Date	24 hour average concentration		
	Lead (μg/m^3)	Nickel (ng/m^3)	Arsenic (ng/m^3)

Analyst **Supervisor** **Incharge**

REFERENCES

Aerosol Science & Technology: The PM 2.5 Federal Reference Method (FRM)." 35(4): 339-342

BIS Method IS 5182 (Part 12): 2004

CARB SOP MLD 055

EPA compendium method IO 3

EPA compendium method IO 3.1

EPA compendium method IO 3.2

Federal Register/Vol. 72, No. 112/Tuesday, June 12, 2007/Rules and Regulations

Indophenol method (Method 401, Air Sampling and Analysis, 3rd Edition), Lewis Publishers Inc.

IS 5182 Part 6 Methods for Measurement of Air Pollution: Oxides of Nitrogen.

IS 5182 Part 23 Method of Measurement of Air Pollution: Respirable Suspended Particulate Matter (PM10) Cyclonic Flow Technique.

IS 5182 Part 23 Method of Measurement of Air Pollution: Respirable Suspended Particulate Matter (PM_{10}) cyclonic flow technique.

Method 501, Air Sampling and Analysis, 3rd Edition, Lewis publishers Inc.

Method IO-2.1 Sampling of Ambient Air for Total Suspended Particulate Matter (SPM) and PM_{10} Using High Volume (HV) Sampler.

Method IO-2.1 Sampling of Ambient Air for Total Suspended Particulate Matter (SPM) and PM10 Using High Volume (HV) Sampler

Method 501, Air Sampling and Analysis, 3rd Edition, Lewis publishers Inc.

Method 411, Air Sampling and Analysis, 3rd Edition (Determination of Oxidizing Substances in the Atmosphere)

40 CFR Parts 53 and 58 Revised Requirements for Designation of Reference and Equivalent Methods for PM2.5 and Ambient Air Quality Surveillance for Particulate Matter; Final Rule.

$PM_{2.5}$ Gravimetric Analysis - Revision 7, August 14, 2003, Page 2 of 24 RTI (Research Triangle Institute, US)

USEPA Method TO-13

Standard Method-American Public Health Association (APHA), 20th Edition, 1998.

Index

❑❑❑❑❑❑